THE SOMETIMES WHY

THE SOMETIMES WHY

Short Stories, Monologues, and
Words to That Effect

DANIEL T BROWN

To order additional copies of this book, contact:
Xlibris
844-714-8691
www.Xlibris.com
Orders@Xlibris.com
815417

CONTENTS

THE ROLEX TUDOR PRINCE OYSTERDATE WITH STEEL BLUE DIAL

PICTURE a seven-year-old me kneeling at a coffin. My head down like I was praying. My grandfather's viewing. I was terrified. It had to be the first dead person I'd ever seen. I lifted my chin and dared myself to open my eyes. Doing anything to make sure my gaze never caught a glimpse of his face, I focused on his hands; more specifically the watch on his wrist. Gold dial . . . beautiful blue face; the day of the month at the three o'clock mark, and a worn, brown leather band. I was fascinated with the thin, gold second hand ticking over Tudor Prince Oysterdate lettering. Why was the watch still running? Why would Grandpa go to heaven with a running watch? Sadly the concept of symbolism was lost on my seven-year-old intellect.

What I remember thinking was that it had to be wrong to bury him with a watch that was still working like that. I convinced myself that maybe it was a mistake. So I reached into the box and took it right off his stiff, dead hand. What the hell? I didn't even look out to notice if anyone had seen me. With my fingertips, I carefully grabbed at the tiny buckle on the band and unfastened it. I was doing everything possible to avoid touching his skin, but occasionally I'd feel the dead flesh against my own. I cringed.

I got up with the watch concealed in my palms. Suddenly I was overcome with fear and regret. I rushed to the ladies' room. I sat in the stall shaking, fighting for air. Maybe I was going to die. I'll put it back. But how? The bathroom door swings open and my Aunt Elaine rushes in. She's crying inconsolably. My mom comes in to comfort her. Through the slat opening in the stall, I can see Aunt Elaine sobbing, crying in my mother's arms. Tears in my mother's eyes . . . missing their dad.

All the while I'm gripping the dead man's watch.

When they pulled themselves together and left, I shoved it in my coat pocket, and when I got home I tucked it in my dresser in the pajama draw, second from the top. Returning the watch never got another thought. Too risky . . . too selfish. It would be my little dark secret.

One afternoon I came home from school and my father was sitting on the couch. It was weeks after the funeral. He was just sitting there staring at me as I made my way into the living room and put down my books. He motioned for me to come and sit with him. On the wrist he waved me over with, he was wearing the watch. I remember resigning myself to the fact that punishment of some manner was imminent. But guess what? It turns out that my dad felt the same way that I did about the watch going to waste in a casket. He tells me the only reason they were going to bury Grandpa with the Rolex Tudor Prince Oysterdate with the steel blue dial in the first place was that his daughters, Aunt Elaine and my mom, were at war over who got to keep it after the old man dropped. And now it would forever belong to our side of the family. Now it was our dark secret. I had done good.

My birthday is February 29. The family would always celebrate on March 1 on non-leap years. But 1980 was a leap year, I remember. And for my eighth birthday, we went to Disney World.

The night before we left for Orlando, I was woken really late by my parents fighting. They fought their share, but this was bigger and louder. They were in the backyard. My dad had a shovel. He had dug a hole in the yard lawn. I watched my mother place something in the hole he dug. The watch.

The secret unraveled when my mother found a pawnshop receipt in his pants pocket. A receipt for the Rolex Tudor Prince Oysterdate with the steel blue dial. Dad pleaded with my mother that I had stolen it and not him, and he was just pawning it for extra vacation money to make me happy. I went right under the bus. My mother dragged him to the shop to pull it out of hock. The backyard scene was a second attempt at getting the watch in the ground.

After the station wagon was packed in the morning, my mother called a family meeting. Mom went on to explain that the Rolex had been a gift that my grandfather had received from my grandmother when he returned from Vietnam. For bravery and being wounded, Grandpa was to receive a Purple Heart. Believing that he was just "doing his job," he didn't take the medal. Grandma got him the gold watch with the steel blue face as a more subtle recognition of the hero he was in her eyes. A watch, the colors of the Purple Heart, or close enough. Symbolism.

Grandpa passed when he succumbed to the effects of Agent Orange. When things had become terminal, my grandmother asked Aunt Elaine and my mom to get together and have the watch fixed and refurbished. The sisters pitched in for the cost. That's why it was running in the coffin. The shit my dad fed me about the sisters fighting over the watch never happened.

Before the three of us got in the car for my guilt-filled trip to Disney World, my father suggested that we not let this "unfortunate" turn of events ruin our trip. That turned out to be the equivalent of asking Mary Todd Lincoln to try and not let her husband's assassination ruin what was otherwise a wonderful theater experience.

Those were the last words, excuse me, the last civil words my parents would ever exchange. The last words were exchanged during a shit storm fight that my parents had in front of the Magic Kingdom. I still wake from nightmares and the visual of Snow White standing between my mother and father, trying to keep them apart as they hurled f-bombs at one another. Grumpy ran and got security, and we were removed from the park.

My father drove me back to New York. My mother flew back ahead of us.

During the ride back, I asked my father why he lied to me about my mom and Aunt Elaine fighting over the watch. My father said the truth is a "tricky thing." Sometimes the truth hurts people and creates unnecessary trouble. He said more times than not, the truth is just another problem people don't need.

At that moment I took what he was saying to mean that he lied to keep me from feeling guilty about what I had done. The more I learned about the man as I got older, the more I learned about his interesting relationship with the truth. By the time the car pulled up to the house, my father's stuff was packed on the porch.

I must have apologized to my mother a million times over the years for what I'd done. What I would come to realize is that my mother wasn't hanging on to the disappointment I was to her, but the disappointment she was to her mother.

Burying her husband with the watch meant the world to my grandmother. But it was all taken away because of me and a moment of thoughtlessness and selfishness. My mother made a full confession to her family. Through no fault of her own, my mother learned the important lesson that there are some wounds that an "I'm sorry" won't heal.

Grandma never did much to hide the fact that she did not forgive my mother or her corpse-robbing daughter. Aunt Elaine went to an early grave having not spoken to my mother for a good twenty years.

Almost a year ago, my mother went into assisted living. The signs of dementia were apparent long before the diagnosis confirmed all suspicions.

One night at the end of one of my visits, Mom said the words, "Rolex Tudor Prince Oysterdate with the steel blue dial." Where did that come from? She remembered the watch, and she told me she was looking for it. I reminded her that it had been buried with her father. She and Aunt Elaine took care of everything, and their mother was so proud of them.

Before disappearing back into the dark of her disease, my mother closed her eyes and smiled a big, big smile. "That's nice," she said.

It's a tricky thing.

FROM MONTCLAIR TO MEMPHIS

I N 1991 my family made the drive from Montclair to Memphis. It was two weeks earlier that my Aunt Rosemary had gone to "meet the Lord," as Pastor Frank put it. The trip to Graceland was a request Rosemary made of my dad from the bed in which death claimed her.

Dad said it only seemed right that our family experience Graceland, a place that had brought his newly departed sister so much joy over the years. For her the King of Rock 'n' Roll was as much a symbol of America as the stars and stripes.

Aunt Rosemary saw Elvis as a symbol of freedom, rebellion, love, and kindness. She knew in her heart that Elvis Aaron Presley was a gift from God to America—a reward for saving the world from Nazi tyranny a decade earlier.

At family gatherings, Rosemary would describe the king's home to us in the way television preachers describe the kingdom of heaven. Admittedly I had not seen a whole lot of the world as a fifteen-year-old in the spring of '91. Yet, I found myself completely on board with my late aunt's assessment of casa de Elvis as my parents led me through the iron gates bearing musical notes and silhouettes of the man from Tupelo.

I don't know if you've ever been to Graceland, but each room in the home is a stop along the tour. You stand at the entrance, and there's a guide who recites a short speech about Elvis' experience with the room.

The Trophy Room is a massive space, and there are gold records hanging on the walls all the way up to the ceiling. I remember taking in how remarkable this room was as my dad pulled me in front of him for a better look, and Mom took pictures.

"The Trophy Room was where Elvis would often come to think, meditate, or compose music," the guide recited. "On the evening of August 16, 1977, Elvis came to this room alone with a guitar. He strummed the chords to 'Love Me Tender' and 'How Great Thou Art' before retiring to bed and dying in his sleep."

The room fell quiet as we took in the moment. Then, almost out of nowhere, a boy around eight or nine raised his hand.

"I thought that Elvis died in the bathroom," the kid said.

Awkwardness claimed the room. However, the guide remained completely unfazed.

"The Trophy Room was where Elvis would often come to think, meditate, or compose music," the words were repeated. "On the evening of August 16, 1977, Elvis came to this room alone with a guitar. He strummed the chords to 'Love Me Tender' and 'How Great Thou Art' before retiring to bed and dying in his sleep."

As this inquisitive boy had yet to learn the value of leaving well enough alone, he continued to make his case. This time he invoked a witness.

"But Dad, you said that Elvis died sitting on the toilet," the boy exclaimed while pulling on his father's jacket sleeve, seeking validation. By now nervous laughter from a few of our fellow tourists became part of the mix.

The guide's volume and inflection didn't waiver the third time around. "The Trophy Room was where Elvis would often come to think, meditate, or compose music. On the evening of August 16, 1977, Elvis came to this room alone with a guitar. He strummed the chords to

'Love Me Tender' and 'How Great Thou Art' before retiring to bed and dying in his sleep."

This standoff, and seemingly time itself, had reached an impasse. Our tour guide ushered the group on to the next room under a dense cloud of discomfort.

Later I stood with my parents by the stables and watched the Graceland horses feed. Mom put her arm around my dad, who placed his hand on my shoulder and led us through the Lord's Prayer. Mom pulled a white and blue flowered vase from her bag and handed it to him. My mother turned and walked me toward a gift shop. I took a quick look back at my father. I saw him pouring what appeared to be sand and dust out of the vase onto the grass at the fence that kept the horses.

Over dinner in the hotel restaurant, I asked my parents about the incident in the Graceland Trophy Room. I wanted to know who had been telling the truth about Elvis Presley's death.

"You know what your grandpa used to say about the truth," Dad turned toward me and asked. "He'd say that the truth is like a wet dog scratching at your backdoor, trying to get out of the rain. Sure, the right thing to do is let the dog in. But knowing that he's going to turn your house into a wet, muddy mess makes you think hard about pretending he's not there. Turn the music up loud enough, and soon you find yourself doubting that you ever heard him, to begin with."

We returned home in time to attend a mass in Aunt Rosemary's honor at St. Luke's. Afterward, we all went back to our house. Over drinks and food, friends and relatives took turns telling stories and paying tribute to Rosemary. Those gathered in our living room were very much in agreement that her blood, sweat, and tears were the glue that held our family together.

When it was my father's turn, he stood up and raised his glass. "To my darling sister Rosemary. Her love and admiration for God, country, and of course the King of Rock 'n' Roll were only exceeded by her love of family. May God welcome her into heaven to be reunited with her husband Lonnie, the man she lived for and missed so dearly."

Just as he finished his toast, my father's attention was stolen by a young woman who was watching quietly from across the room.

"Why are you here?" my father asked with pain and anger in his voice.

"She was my mother," the woman responded.

Having never met my cousin Lisa, I had no way of knowing who she was until she identified herself.

"You broke your mother's heart and sent her to an early grave with your evil lies and horrible accusations," my father continued. "You have no right."

"I didn't come to make trouble," Lisa answered while taking in stares from the room of mourners. "I thought maybe coming might bring about some peace."

"You're not welcome here," my father pointed at Lisa. "You're not welcome in this family."

"What I said my father did is true, and my mother let it happen," Lisa's voice cracked. "The only lie is everyone pretending that I don't exist."

"Rosemary would never allow such a thing," my father rested his case. "Not my sister."

He demanded that Lisa leave our home. As my cousin walked to the sidewalk, I ran up behind her. I tried to explain away my father's anger, and Lisa said she understood. Lisa said she realized coming by was a mistake. I asked her what she and my father were talking about.

Lisa pulled a letter from her jacket pocket and handed it to me. I unfolded the paper and read the handwritten message to Lisa from my Uncle Lonnie. The letter was an apology to Lisa, and a heartfelt admission of guilt. Uncle Lonnie confessed to the horrible things he had done. Things that robbed Lisa of her childhood. Lonnie had violated Lisa, and the letter was a desperate attempt to unburden himself of the shame and guilt he carried. In the letter, he begged for her forgiveness for what he had done. He hated himself for driving her away from her home and the family whose job it was to love and protect her.

Lisa told me to hold on to the letter. She hoped that maybe someday I could show it to my father, and he could begin to understand the truth . . . for better or for worse.

One spring evening, weeks later, I approached my father in his bedroom. He was listening to Elvis on the CD player, "How Great Thou Art." I was holding my cousin's letter in my hand. I asked my father about what went on between Lonnie and Lisa. My father was quick to reject my line of inquiry. He said that he had heard the rumors a long time ago. My father said that he had asked Rosemary about it, and she swore that Lisa was lying. She and Uncle Lonnie said it was all made up.

I presented the letter that Lisa had given me. I tried to show it to my father, but he wouldn't look. Instead, he reached out and raised the volume of the music. "But Dad . . .," I tried to reason with him. I wanted him to hear me. But each time I spoke, he raised the volume even louder, and the words of Elvis overtook my own. Eventually, I surrendered. I fell silent and noticed that raindrops were starting to land on the bedroom window that looked out onto the night. At that moment I thought I heard the cries of a small animal, a dog perhaps, pawing at the back door. But the music made it difficult to discern. Maybe I had only imagined what I'd heard.

At the time, I found my father's denial confusing. As a young girl, I came to see the truth as a tonic that made everything all right—an elixir that put life and the world in its proper place. It took me years to understand. One or two doses of harsh reality, which required a sugary spoonful of denial for me to digest.

And why not? When you get down to it, to the realness, life's true bottom line—is reality so wonderful that it deserves our full attention? Can't we just wish away the undesirable memories that stand in the way of our peace of mind? Are we so at fault for trying?

Don't we have the right to remember our loved ones and embrace the legacy of our heroes in the manner that brings us joy and makes us smile?

For some of us, the sun shines so much brighter and the air smells so much sweeter when Elvis is remembered as a rock-and-roll idol who died at peace in Memphis with his head on a pillow and "Love Me Tender" in his heart. And for a small group of everyday people from Montclair, New Jersey, the world is a better place when my Aunt Rosemary is remembered as the ideal wife and mother, who ascended to the afterlife, dancing on heaven's streets of gold to the sounds of "Blue Suede Shoes," and so much more than a pile of dust and ashes at the foot of the stable fence at Graceland.

MELROSE

M Y problem is that I try to come up with something clever to say when he's being an asshole. Ben goes right for the heart, and I'm searching for witty sarcasm and clever comebacks when a "go fuck yourself" would do just fine.

We had just gotten home from the emergency room. I was not in the mood. And there's a line he's dying to use on me. Benjamin is biting his tongue, and I know it's coming. Instead, he goes for the C-word: "crazy." Let's not get crazy. Which is code for me not to get crazy. Which always makes me insane.

Yes, I have issues. I own that, and I'm in therapy. Actually, I'm seeing two therapists. Then again, one is a therapist I see, the other is part of an online therapy program I signed up for. We just email each other, so technically I'm not seeing him.

But Benjamin's nonsense isn't helping. Not at a moment when my thoughts were focused on how serious the accident was. Would there be permanent damage, scarring, disfigurement? How much guilt would I be carrying with me from now on?

Then he says the line he's been holding back: "Jesus, Margaret . . . It's just a goddamn cat." I turn red. I smell his fear as he tries to walk it back. "I just don't like to see you upset." Benjamin retreats. "I bet it's nothing that serious anyway."

Let me tell you. When your cat has redness from scratching, it's probably nothing serious. The random cut or bruise . . . not serious. Sure, I'm no doctor. But I'd have to believe that when you show up at the animal hospital with some of your cat in one hand, and the rest of it in another . . . it's something serious. It's definitely that serious.

Melrose isn't just a cat. To me, he's one of the very few life choices I've truly made on my own. I picked him out at the shelter. I was certain that Melrose was the right cat. There was no doubt. He's one of the blanks in my life that I filled in for myself.

If you don't fill in the blanks in your life, life has a way of filling them in for you.

I didn't choose to be a medical technician in a urologist's office. I was out of work. My ex-roommate's friend was leaving the position and she got me in. Six years later this is me. And whether I see myself as an important cog in curing the sick and saving the world, or as a woman pushing thirty who makes her living lugging around jars of old men's piss, and emptying trash cans filled with discarded rubber gloves from prostate exams, depends on which side of the bed I wake up on that day.

And Benjamin? We were set up by mutual friends who thought we'd be perfect for each other. He's not the kind of guy that I would choose for myself. Fair enough, the first date was phenomenal. But every girl eventually learns the lesson that any guy can do at least one good date. Every man has at least one clean shirt, and enough bullshit to sell himself off as "the guy."

But then you get the package home, put on an engagement ring, and find out that the user manual is in ten different languages. Even the English looks like it's written in Klingon, or some other indecipherable dreck.

On more than one occasion he had dropped hints to friends that we're trying to have a baby. When I called him out on it, he said that us being engaged implied that we would be having kids, and that he didn't think it was something that needed its own separate discussion.

Ben's belief was that it was our job to keep his family's legacy and lineage going. I'd just smile and nod. However, having met these people, I'd have to say that chopping down this family tree isn't such a bad idea. Any scientist who doubts that man descended from Neanderthals needs to sit down to the evening meal with these folks.

I've seen *National Geographic* documentaries on primates that eat their young, or baboons that throw feces at each other that show more love and respect for one another than Ben's family. How could he think that I could possibly walk away from a dinner with that collection of the low bar of humanity and come to the conclusion, "Hey! Let's make more of these people."

I'd just go along. Besides, trying to have kids would have to imply that we were actually having sex. Unless Ben's impression was that getting rub and tugs at the Happy Handjob massage parlor was going to get me pregnant.

About six months into our relationship, he moved me into his apartment. Again, not the home I'd pick for myself. But life fills in the blanks. Not truly feeling like this was my home is probably what led to the whole Melrose disaster in the first place. Housework is not my thing—the dust, the dirt . . . it gets overwhelming.

I invested in one of those robotic floor cleaners, the ones that sweep and move around the house on their own. We barely had the thing a week. I turned it on, and Benjamin and I went to have wings and beer with his fantasy football crew at the Blarney. When we got home, the machine had Melrose's front left leg stuck in its gears. Ben smashed it open, I wrapped Melrose in a beach towel, and we took off in the car. We left Melrose at the hospital. I begged the vet to please save his leg.

On the way home, Benjamin took the opportunity to say we needed to be adults about this. Saving Melrose's leg would certainly require surgery. We needed to examine the potential cost and decide whether putting him down would be the better choice.

When I broke down and resisted, he went for my heart. He said I really shouldn't have a say in the matter. After all, I only had myself to blame for this.

That night when I was changing for bed, I took a long look in the bathroom mirror. Who was I? Where was I? And how the hell did I get here?

When did this become all right? When did the girl that believed in her soul that she deserved every good thing life has to offer become someone willing to trade a soul mate, passion, and intensity for a man with a decent dental plan and prescription drug coverage?

I heard my mother's voice telling me that love is hard work. Love and marriage is hard work. But you stick with it. You'll see, it's worth it. No. Love takes no work at all. Forcing yourself to believe you're in love when you're not. That's a full-time job.

I stared down my reflection and asked myself how much more denial was I willing to live in. How many more glasses of wine at dinner, or what dosage of Zoloft would it take to keep this going? At what point did the crutches I used to be able to deal with real life become the tools I use not to deal with it?

The next morning I called the hospital and told them to do everything in their power to make Melrose whole again. Money was not an issue. I told Ben what I had done, and it was game on. He came at me with that "I'm the adult in the room" shit, but it bounced right off me. I let him know that he had no say in what I'd be doing with Melrose. My life choices were not up for discussion, and I had no interest in having a Neanderthal baby.

And one more thing—for saying that Melrose getting hurt was my fault, "Go fuck yourself."

Ben folded his arms and looked at me. "Are you done?" he asked. I returned the look and took a deep breath as I forced the diamond from my right ring finger.

Yes, I said, I'm done.

DANIEL T BROWN

FLESH WOUNDS

THE scene: A crowded, lively wedding reception. A toast has just been made to the bride and groom. Jeanine enters and approaches the man holding the microphone.

Excuse me! Excuse me. Can I have the mic, please?

Jeanine grabs the microphone.

Everybody. Attention please. Everybody please. For God's sake. Here we are at my good friend's wedding reception, and it's only right that I make a toast. Cara O'Reilly. Oh, I'm sorry. It's Cara O'Reilly Mullen now, isn't it? Isn't that beautiful? Cara O'Reilly Mullen, I want to thank you and your lovely Michael for inviting me to your most holy day. The ceremony was magical and wonderful. And it is my sincere hope that every day forward for you both is filled with moments that are just as magical and just as wonderful. Let's give them a hand. That is how I truly feel . . . from the heart, people.

And I hope I am not crossing any boundaries by coming up here like this. I mean, I'm not the maid of honor. Hey, I wasn't even chosen to be in the wedding party. Really? But that's okay. It's not like it was a surprise. After all, I wasn't in the wedding party for Cara O'Reilly Mullen's first nuptials either.

Wait, back then it was Cara O'Reilly McCarthy, wasn't it? Who knows, maybe the third time will be the charm for me. You know, it's not like we grew up together as next-door neighbors. Am I right? It's not like I was the only one who would hang out in gym class with Cara in freshmen year when word got out that she has inverted nipples.

And while I have everyone's attention, there's another elephant in the room that needs to be addressed. By now it's painfully clear that I am here by myself. Like for so many wonderful occasions we've shared over the years, I was unable to secure a date. Yes, I'm at my best friend's wedding unescorted. Stag. Solo. I'm here with a plus zero. I only bring this up because things were supposed to different today. I actually RSVP'd for two. But as we know, Jeanine makes plans and God laughs. Oh, does God laugh.

You know, I used to dream of happily ever after. The house, the four-door family car, a wonderful relationship with a man who I could truly call my life mate. Just like Cara O'Reilly Mullen. Time passed and I started to think that maybe, just maybe, I had set my sights too high. Perhaps if I just try to find a husband, someone to share life with—the ups and downs, happiness, tears—maybe then my dreams would be a little more attainable. Then more time passed and I realized that Jeanine was still asking too much.

Lately, I simply set out to find a man to befriend . . . a companion. We could share a few laughs, a bit of romance, the odd dinner date, a movie. But it seems that even this was a bridge too far. However, today was the wedding of a dear friend, and lo and behold, Jeanine is involved with a man in something that somewhat resembles a relationship. This time the chair next to mine would not be occupied by a stranger. Tonight would not be spent on the dance floor trapped in the embrace of horny, elderly, miscreant friends and relatives of the bride and groom, who are offering a pity dance to a lonely lady. And as the night grew older, the intoxicating effects of desperation and free alcohol would lead to uninvited sneaking and groping hands invading my most cherished physical assets. And what had started as friendly pecks on the cheek from Grandpa would devolve into full-out open-mouth-and-tongue assaults. All of which would leave me with overwhelming feelings of self-loathing, disgust, and sometimes even—and I say this with no shame—arousal.

But tonight was going to be different. Yet, as you can see, I stand before you just a few more glasses of champagne away from shaking what the good Lord gave me to the thumping beat of the Electric Slide with Uncle Seamus' benign manhood pressed against my thigh.

Full disclosure, I wasn't exactly stood up. Eddie said he would try to meet me here . . . if he can get the bleeding to stop. Bleeding, you ask? Well, ten minutes before he was supposed to pick me up, Eddie called to say he's running late because . . . he'd been shot. There was a shootout involving the police. But not to worry, it's only a flesh wound. Eddie didn't want to ruin my good time, so he insisted that I go on without him.

But today isn't about me, is it? It's about good ol' Cara O'Reilly McCarthy Mullen. So let's raise our glasses to the bride and groom.

Jeanine raises her glass then has second thoughts.

And just in case you're wondering, Eddie isn't a cop. Actually, I'm kinda out of the loop when it comes to what the man is up to. Eddie says it's best that I don't know how he makes his money. From what I can gather, it involves cough medicine, cow manure, and lighter fluid. So my closest guess is that he either runs a meth lab, or he's working with Gwyneth Paltrow and the Goop brand on some cure for dryness of the lady parts.

So here's to you, Cara O'Reilly McCarthy Mullen and Michael O'Reilly McCarthy Mullen Cougar Mellencamp.

Before Jeanine can raise her glass, another thought interrupts her.

And how about that ceremony? What were the vows that Cara wrote? "Love and life are precious. Neither are promised to us. Rather, they are blessings to be counted and cherished. So in this moment, and for however many moments we may share, Michael, I choose you, and I choose love."

That there is gold. Those words mean something, people.

Actually, hearing that reminded me of a time when I thought I had met "The Guy." We were introduced through a dating site for Jewish singles. May God strike me dead, it's the only time I've ever denounced Jesus Christ as my Lord and Savior. But me and this guy hit it off great online. But when we met in person, the date went nowhere. So we got trashed. I paid, of course. Anything to drown out the awkward silence. So he walks me home from this disaster of a date, and it's snowing out and all. We get to my building and say goodnight. I'm walking up the outside stairs and I hear this noise. I turn around and this guy has his wang out, and he's peeing into the snow on the sidewalk. So uninhibited. And just like that, I get it. I'm like, holy shit, here's a guy who's not afraid to go for it. No caution. No fear. This was the guy I fell in love with over text messages. With that I seized the moment, and before he could zip up, I brought him up to my apartment. We rapped nasties 'til sunrise. He never returned any of my calls after that. Still it taught me a lot about myself and how to live my life.

Ladies and gentlemen, these are the moments we must cherish. Please fill your glasses, raise them high with me, and let's . . .

Jeanine raises her glass once more. However, the vibrating phone in her dress cleavage steals her attention.

Hold on. I have to take this.

Jeanine answers her phone and responds to the caller.

Oh. Oh no. Really? Okay . . . okay. I'll be right there.

Jeanine returns her attention to the reception guests.

That was the hospital. They have Eddie. The doctors don't expect him to make it. The bullet nicked an artery, and it's way more serious than Eddie had thought.

But get this. Eddie asked the nurses to call me. When he found out he was going to die, he told them to ask if I could come and be by his side. His last request was to die in my arms. Here's a man who resisted sharing even the most basic details of his life. But he chose to share his death with me. It's so beautiful. I have to go. The man I love needs me to watch him die.

Jeanine takes a step to exit. She stops, turns, and raises her glass.

"Love and life are precious. Neither are promised to us. Rather, they are blessings to be counted and cherished. So in this moment, and for however many moments we may share, Eddie, I choose you, and I choose love." Here's to you, Michael Mullen and Cara O'Reilly Mullen. It is to your happiness that we drink.

Jeanine drinks her full glass then exits.

SIX LOST DAYS IN NOVEMBER

IN the summer of '76, I was riding in my Uncle Reggie's car with my Aunt Shea and cousin Rainey. We were coming home from Five Towns when we saw this car pulled off to the side of the road. The car had hit a divider. The thing was totaled and the driver was stuck in the vehicle. Oil and fluids were leaking onto the ground, and the driver was desperately trying to pull himself out of the window.

Aunt Shea asked Reggie if we should pull over to help. Uncle Reggie kept driving. He said there was nothing we could do. Rainey and I looked at each other, then looked away. It was so unsettling. But rather than taking in what we saw, we acted like what was happening wasn't happening.

"When you see a guy that's so deep in the mess, the best you can do is say a prayer and light a candle for him," Reggie said. "The next time I'm in church, that's what I'll do."

As a little girl, my parents sent me to spend summers with my Uncle Reggie and Aunt Shea at their house in Rockaway Beach. Next to the front door on their porch was a dirty white wooden sign with faded black lettering that read, "Help Wanted—Irish Need Not Apply." Aunt Shea hated the sign and was after Uncle Reggie to get rid of it. She said it was a reminder of a hurtful time in our heritage, and there was no need for it. "Over my dead body," Reggie would boast. "That sign is a reminder of where our people came from. Let us never forget that no man is any better, or any worse, than another."

Reggie's claim to fame as far as advocating for diversity and acceptance of others was that he fully accepted the Puerto Rican family on the three-hundred block and never "held the fact that they were Spanish" against them. Aunt Shea had long ago given up on trying to explain to her beloved that being Puerto Rican and being Spanish wasn't the same thing. Given the fact that this family was actually from Ecuador made the whole effort seem fruitless to Aunt Shea anyway.

The year I turned ten my parents split, and I found myself living with Reggie and Shea permanently. All parties, me included, decided this was for the best. That fall I was registered to start fifth grade at St. Camillus. Rainey had told her parents that I was nervous about moving to a new school and meeting new people. Shea sat me down and told me that there was nothing to be afraid of. She said that I have a wonderful heart, and that's what counts. Aunt Shea said to never cheapen myself by trying to be something that I'm not just to gain favor with others.

Reggie jumped in and corrected his wife. "You might as well learn this when you're young. What you are in this life is not important. It's all about who you want to be. Live your life like you're someone special, like you got it all figured out. Plan for something big, and something big will come. Go into that school and show them that you're a somebody before anyone ever gets a chance to tell you you're a nobody. That's what the winners in life do."

To be fair to Uncle Reggie, this was a bit of his own advice that he actually took. "We get by here. Food is on the table and there're clothes on our backs," he'd say. "But in my heart, and in my mind, I'm a millionaire."

Whenever Reggie went into his "I'm a millionaire in my heart" rant, Aunt Shea would do the sign of the cross and mutter, "Jesus, here we go." The whole millionaire dream idea came to Reggie in the early '80s when a man named Lou Eisenberg became the first person to win millions playing the New York Lottery. Reggie would cut all the articles out of the papers about Lou Eisenberg. "This is going to be me!" he'd say.

Reggie's strategy was simple, albeit a bit bizarre. He only played the dollar game every week—a single ticket. The numbers he played were our house number, his birthday, Aunt Shea's birthday, Rainey's and my birthday together . . . thirty-four, the jersey number of his favorite Mets player, Mookie Wilson, and the birthday of, believe it or not, Engelbert Humperdinck. Yes, the singer Engelbert Humperdinck. Engelbert was born on May 2, so the number two was part of his six magic numbers. Don't ask me why.

As our time together went on, Shea and Reggie began finding it harder and harder to not fight in front of us. Reggie would storm out sometimes, and Rainey and I would ask where Reggie was. Shea would say he's in his office, which meant he was throwing back Rheingolds at the Irish Circle.

Another Reggie-ism was, "He's a shirt-off-his-back guy." That meant that he was talking about someone that would literally give the shirt off his back to you if needed. He'd do anything for you.

Tim Mullen was a friend of Reggie's who lived off Executive Boulevard in Yonkers. Tim was a "shirt-off-the-back guy" as Reggie saw it. In November of 1982, Reggie told Shea that he got an emergency call from Timmy, and needed to get up to Yonkers right away.

With no explanation, and not much more than an "I'm sorry," one Monday morning Uncle Reggie took off for a week in Yonkers. He missed Thanksgiving. To this day no one besides Reggie himself knows exactly where he was or what he was doing. Shea always referred to that experience as the "Six Lost Days in November."

Even as little kids we could see that Aunt Shea saw Reggie as a fool. And the way she saw it, if she had promised her life to a fool, what did that make her? She took it so personally . . . felt so much anger and shame. Shea had no friends. She never invited guests to her home; the phone never rang. It was as if she was tormented by the fact that she had hitched her wagon to a man who stood on the wrong side of every issue, and never passed up an opportunity to show his ignorance. Now she was facing middle age with the realization that her life was dedicated to a man who was betting his future on the one-in-a-trillion chance that someday the winning combination of lottery numbers would reflect our birthdays, house number, Mookie goddam Wilson's jersey, and the birthday of Engel- fucking-bert Humperdinck.

But it happened. It actually happened.

The winning numbers drawn for the New York State Lottery on November 27, 1982, were 1– Mookie Wilson; 2 – You-know-who's birthday; 9 – Shea's birthday in June; 16 – Reggie's October birthday; 34 – me and Rainey's birthday; and 40 – our house number.

As coincidence would have it, the drawing took place on the fifth of Reggie's lost days. We hadn't even watched the drawing. The news that Reggie's numbers came in got to our door when a small group of his drinking buddies came calling and asked if they could congratulate the town's new millionaire.

Shea tried calling Tim Mullen's number, but it just rang without anyone picking up. Rainey and I saw how excited Shea was. "I can't believe it," she said. "I think your Uncle Reggie's done it. I think we're rich."

It would be almost another full day before Reggie returned. Shea was feeding Rainey and I dinner on Saturday when we heard Reggie's key turn the front door lock.

Shea rushed to meet Reggie in the foyer. She led him to the couch and sat him down. Reggie started spewing apologies for leaving and not calling. He began rambling about promising to be a better husband and father.

"You don't know . . . do you?" Shea asked.

Reggie didn't get a chance to answer before Shea jumped in again. "Reginald. Look at me. Did you play your numbers this week?"

Reggie smiled a big smile. "No. That's what I wanted to tell you," he said. "I'm giving up on that nonsense. Timmy set me straight. I realized how foolish I was being. I'm a new man. From now on."

Shea stood up, and she handed him a piece of paper that had been given to her by the men who showed up the night before. On the paper were the winning numbers, and a congratulations message from the guys.

Shea came back to the table and sat with us in silence. Reggie just sat on the couch in his coat and hat, staring into nowhere.

The lottery jackpot was five million dollars. One winning ticket was sold. The entire five million was won by a man from Newark named Curtis Sharp; a cool black guy in a three-piece suit and bowler hat. The day he came forward to claim the prize, he showed up with his wife on one arm and his girlfriend on the other.

Curtis Sharp became a national celebrity. Reggie was left sitting on his recliner with the loose spring that pinched his back when he leaned too far to the right, watching Curtis on TV sitting with Johnny Carson, and doing interviews on every channel. There was Curtis Sharp living Uncle Reggie's dream on the front page of the *Daily News* posing for pictures with Andy Warhol.

To know my Uncle Reggie is to know that there is no tragedy or life catastrophe that he can't make worse. To try to make up for the missed opportunity, he began playing the lottery with every dollar he could get his hands on. He just played random numbers; he begged and borrowed. Reggie said if he could pick the winning numbers once, he could surely do it twice. He never came close to winning again.

It all caught up with him when loan sharks came to our door to threaten him in front of all of us. Not long after that, our electricity got shut off due to a lack of payment to LILCO.

Uncle Reggie and Aunt Shea seemed to get old very quickly in the passing years. Somewhere along the way, Rainey went from being the daughter to being the caretaker for her parents.

When I was barely seventeen, I got the hell out. I got engaged to a guy that worked the admissions booth at the Playland amusement park, and we made plans to drive to California and get into movies.

Last November Aunt Shea went on to her reward. I stopped by the house a few weeks later and Rainey was going over finances with Reggie. He was looking at bankruptcy. Rainey made arrangements for Reggie to move into an adult-care facility.

After a long silence to take in the idea of moving into a nursing home, Reggie agreed. But he insisted he would only have to live there for a little while until he saved some money that he could put on some stocks he'd had his eye on. Eventually, he would be able to cash out and buy the house in Maui he always dreamed of. Reggie said he would find his way back and finally become that millionaire.

Rainey and I looked at each other, then looked away. It was so unsettling. But rather than taking in what we saw, we acted like what was happening wasn't happening.

When you see a guy that's so deep in a mess, the best you can do is say a prayer and light a candle for him. The next time I'm in church, that's what I'll do.

JACK THE RIVER

JACK the River
      Waiting for a moment
Wants to start a movement
From his second-story bedroom

Twenty-two with rage and rebel soul
Puts the chair in forward
Rolls up to the window
Sweat rolls across his eyelids
He peers between the dusty metal slats

What used to be a view of the sunset in the sand
Songbirds on the dune
Footprints on the shore
Replaced by endless windows
Brick-and-mortar housing
Higher than the flood plain
Safe from rushing tides

Jack looks in upon the neighbors . . . strangers
Unwelcome in their private moments
Spies their love and anger
Victories and failures
Tears, regrets, and climax
A tidal surge intrusion in their every day

And the river's running dry these days
Years of poison and pollution

Stagnant, murky, frozen in winter
The nets of reckless fishermen captured what was life

Sophia checks the oven
A sheet of rainbow cookies
Smothered in frosting of maternal love
A recipe she knows so well

She reminds herself of sunshine
Walking hand in hand with Jack
Ice cream on the boardwalk
And the river was clear and blue
Robust with the possible

Many would wade into the river
And marvel at its bounty
Before the diagnosis
That turned the water shallow
And made the river toxic

Jack curls a broken fist
Asks his God for the direction home
To when the sun turned the waters gold
Before the people walked away
Before he was recognized as strange
And they labeled him as wrong
Then named him Jack the River

NEW YEAR'S EVE 2012

I AM so not wanting to do this.

Are you recording? Don't record me, I don't want that.

This is private. And don't write down what I'm saying. This is very personal.

All of this can be traced back to a single moment. It's that moment of awakening that comes to those of us who've been sleepwalking through life. The moment we discover that we've been living in a lion's cage. But it's too late, because the paws are already on your chest and the teeth are at your throat.

This moment for me happened on New Year's Eve 2012. For my money there is no greater "what the fuck" moment than counting down from ten as the ball drops, with tears and mascara pouring down your cheeks, surrounded by nurses, police, and hospital security.

Just a few moments earlier I had been making my case that I was the sane one, and everyone else was out of their minds. However, it's very hard to get people to see your side of things when you're the one on a gurney wearing restraints, a paper gown, and a diaper.

The truth that was buried beneath the pile of bullshit that I called my life was that I was insane. The truth was that I was starting off 2013 facing attempted murder charges.

Things between me and David, David and I, were never "normal." But that was the hook. The left-of-center nature was what drew me in to him. It was like being in a special relationship made me special. Believe me, I know it sounds moronic when I say it out loud.

I took David not being overly affectionate or physical as a sign of respect. I'd been through my share of marathon bangs and fuck buddies, so the change made me feel like we were connected on deeper levels. To David I was a partner . . . an equal.

Our most intimate moments came when we shared in our mutual passion for activism and advocating for human rights causes: racial equality, equal pay in the workplace, wind energy, LGBT rights.

We would come back from a rally or demonstration and we were so in love. We were on a high. Then it would be me that tried to push it into the bedroom. Things would either fall apart, or the session would end before anyone finished. Why didn't I speak up? Of course, I blamed myself. I'm the turn-off.

There needs to be a release somewhere, and eventually the fighting started. Before either of us knew it, we became like those fish, the fighting fish—the ones that they have to put dividers between the bowls to keep them from trying to tear each other apart. For me and David, it was a wall of bullshit . . . arguments and bullshit debates. Anything rather than deal with what was really going on.

You know, the fights that keep you distracted from talking about what the real issue is. It's so much easier to say you're hogging the fucking remote than it is to ask why you lose your hard-on whenever you're inside me.

We made it a full year in October. Strangely enough, Thanksgiving and Christmas were actually pretty good. It sounds crazy, but we were still talking about the future. The word "marriage" was being thrown around. I'm sure you assume that I was pushing it, but getting married was David's idea.

The first time I met Charles was at a diner on the lower west side. He met with me and David to get us on board for a gay rights march in DC Thanksgiving weekend. Charles' roommate was in the army reserve, and he was building a discrimination case against the government for unfair treatment of homosexuals on base.

The four of us wound up getting arrested at the Capital. When we got back to New York, Charles and David met several times without me. The plan was for a New Year's Eve demonstration at Times Square. I would drive back from my parents' place in Fishkill. I'd meet David for dinner, and we'd head into Manhattan.

I got back to our apartment early so I could grab a quick shower before dinner. I walk through the front door, and I can see movement in the bedroom right away. I step up into the room and there's David and Charles . . . in our bed.

I had never been in a rage before. I'd never been in a fistfight . . . I always run from confrontation. I don't know what happened. It wasn't my fault.

We all stayed there silent. I couldn't breathe. I clenched my fist. I said . . . You fucking faggot . . .

That's not me. I swear. That's not me. I was devastated and I just grabbed the sharpest weapon I could find.

Please promise me that you are not writing any of this down.

They both just looked at me. We were all in shock. David had such a look of disappointment in his eyes. Like he had just discovered something shocking about me. I'm telling you that there's no dirtier feeling than catching your boyfriend with another guy's dick in his mouth, and I've ceded the moral high ground.

They were in our fucking bed!

DANIEL T BROWN

I stormed out and got back in my car. I took off. I was still seeing red. I get a couple of blocks away and I decide to turn back. I wasn't going to let him get away with making me hate myself.

As I come back down our block, I see David at the curb as Charles is pulling away in a car service. In my head, I think I'm going to scare the shit out of him. But I snapped and I came at him full speed. It wasn't anything human.

He ran back toward the entrance. But he slips and falls. I have him dead to rights.

Suddenly I come out of it and swerve. I swear I missed killing him by inches. I careen into a lamp pole. I don't know if I blacked out or was knocked out.

My next memory is sitting in handcuffs, being driven off in a police car. I look up and David is staring through the car window at me. Like he was trying to figure out who the hell I was.

By the time they got me to the psych ward, I had managed to add assaulting a doctor and resisting arrest as garnish to the main course of my attempted murder charge.

I pleaded guilty to reckless endangerment and the resisting charge. The doctor didn't pursue anything. I got five years' probation and enough fines and fees to keep me scraping my way by for quite a while.

I choose to believe that I'm not capable of murder. But the fact that I was capable of contemplating murder is quite a pill to swallow.

And what about the language I used with David? What does that make me? Do you know that he never even said he was sorry for what I walked in on? Did he think because I was an advocate for the cause that I wouldn't be crushed? I guess he figured at the end of the day we were even.

I accept and own what happened. But what I won't stand for is you judging me. Tell me. In your worst moments, what are *you* capable of? What will you do or say in the moment you're tested?

Ask yourself. And you can write that down.

DANIEL T BROWN

THE BODY AND THE BLOOD

"WE want two sodas . . . no ice. Do you hear me? No ice?"

His voice is raised. His eyes are wide. Walter. He wants me to call him Junior. "People call me Junior," he says.

Well, not me. I refuse to be on a date with a grown man named Junior.

"I'm telling you now, if you bring us sodas with ice, I'm sending the damn things back. You'll bring them right back." The waitress rolls her eyes and walks away with our drink order, and what I'm sure is a deep desire to stab my dinner companion in the eye with a rusty fork.

"That's how they get you," Walter tells me while digging into the breadbasket with his hairy, eczema-laden mitt, ripping into a slice of pumpernickel, pulling it into quarters.

"They fill the glass with ice. This way they're only giving you about half the amount of the drink you're paying for."

This Walter . . . my date . . . is explaining his soda conspiracy theory to me like he's really on to something; like he's discovered the second shooter on the grassy knoll.

I may not believe in love at first sight. But we'd only been out as a couple less than ten minutes and I already know that, from the bottom of my heart, I hate this guy.

Another memorable moment in my latest "alone isn't cutting it" fiasco was Junior telling me how he belongs to this secret society of men who are trying to grow their foreskins back. It's this whole big thing where these morons get together and work to reclaim their primal selves by restoring their foreskins. Junior continued his exercise in too much information on a first date by explaining about his special underwear with weights that attach to his junk and pull the skin forward in an attempt to recreate the uncircumcized state.

From there, Junior went on to share a few more inbred pearls of wisdom such as his belief that Jesus had to be white if he was truly the son of God, and that fibromyalgia is a leftwing scam to give welfare moms an excuse to not work. This allows them to continue sucking on the taxpayers' teat.

All the while I'm sitting there staring right into his eyes and wondering how it could be possible to fit that much asshole into one human being. It's astounding!

I didn't even bother to undress when I got home. I pulled the covers over my head and cursed my life as tears soaked my pillow. Before closing my eyes and succumbing to the effects of Johnny Walker Black and Ambien, I made a commitment to myself that I would not let my fear of being alone coerce me into another waste-of-time relationship. Never again. From now on my standards for romance were going to be more than just a warm body. I deleted his number from my phone and swore off the man named Junior for eternity. From that moment, I affirmed that he was out of my life.

For our second date, Junior took me to see Bob Dylan at the Beacon. During my experience on a ninety-minute contact high, I became acutely aware that the Prophet Zimmerman was, at times, singing directly to me. His words traveled up to the theater balcony, and took shelter in my brain.

Life is sad,
Life is a bust,
All ya can do is do what you must.

I found myself wondering what the moment was when I wandered off the road of normalcy, and onto the path that led to my present life. When did I get separated from the group headed toward the tall, green forest of fulfillment, contentment, and stillness of mind, only to find myself alone wandering in the dreary jungle of crying jags, warm soda, and adjustable underwear hanging from my headboard?

After a spell of deep refection, aided by a hefty inhale of smoke from the monster hash joint being passed freely around us, I found it. I discovered the moment.

Closing my eyes, I was returned to second grade, kneeling in a church pew. It was my first communion. I had already been to the altar and taken the small, white, circular offering between my lips.

In my rush to consume the wafer on my way to return to my seat, I found myself in the precarious predicament of having the communion stuck to the roof of my mouth. I was freaking the hell out. I frantically tried to peel it off with the tip of my tongue. All that did was work the tasteless symbol of the son of God back toward my throat.

With Sister Lenore eyeing our class from the aisle, I didn't dare reach in and touch the clinging wafer with my finger. Mixing my skin with the body of Christ was a one-way ticket to Satan's lair. Asking for her help was also a no-go, for I feared that Sister Lenore would declare in front of everyone that Jesus was rejecting me.

I was terrified that the communion would slide and get stuck in my windpipe, cutting off my air and killing me on the spot. This would leave my spirit with the awkward job of having to appear before the Lord our Father at heaven's gate and explain how I choked to death on his son. But I was spared that indignity when the body of Christ descended into my gullet, surrendering to my digestive tract.

Sure, it's a cute, funny childhood story. Yet, I submit that a direct connection between Jesus stuck to the roof of my mouth, and me stuck in a dead-end pairing with Walter Junior is quite real. Following that bad first communion experience, I became afraid to receive the Eucharist for fear of choking. I had been truly looking forward to being able to receive communion at mass with my friends and family. I was ashamed to admit I was afraid, and I eventually abandoned going to church altogether. Even years later when I would be called out on it, I'd go into some rant about not feeling comfortable with organized religion. But it was all fear that kept me away.

Exhibit B. In eighth grade, Abby Spencer stole my set of colored markers from my book bag. I was furious and walked right up to her and told her to give them back . . . or else! Or else what? Abby asked while standing up from her desk.

Abby said that if I wanted them back, that I would have to take them from her. She told me to meet her after school by the 101st Street deli. She threatened to knock my face bloody. I had braces on my teeth at the time, and all I could imagine was Abby punching my mouth and getting my lips caught on the metal, ripping my face to shreds. Abby was quite a bit smaller than me, but the thought that I would beat her never entered my mind. Projecting negatively in worse-case scenarios had become the norm. Fear.

Surely my markers weren't worth me being disfigured and made ugly for life. I never showed up for the confrontation. Years later Abby would get a scholarship to art school. My greatest accomplishment in the arts was posing nude for a state-sponsored life drawing class in a drug rehab. Some of the guys didn't even bring pads and pencils. They just leered at me as I posed without my clothes on the pedestal. One man tried to tip me. But he walked away mad when I couldn't break a five-dollar bill.

In my lifetime I've beaten alcohol and food addictions . . . cigarettes and compulsive online shopping. But fear is one demon I've never come close to slaying.

For decades I've read self-help books, listened to CDs and podcasts, and taken workshops on overcoming fear. One step forward, two back.

I can't put into words how envious I am of people who take life head-on and never back down to self-doubt. They say "fuck it" to being afraid, and they just go for it. I wish I could. I wish for it so badly.

My cousin Richie was eight years into a career as a firefighter, FDNY. One day he wakes up and decides it's not for him anymore. He quits. Just like that. He buys a pick-up, throws his stuff in, and heads to LA. He wants to try acting. Nothing was set up, no job . . . nothing. He just went. Richie figured it out and he's doing all right. I could never . . .

Cathy—this girl that lives in my building—she's given up on relationships. She swears by Tinder hookups, meeting guys online for one-nighters. She routinely sleeps with three or four guys at any given point without fear. She has a strong sexual appetite, and she does her thing without caring what anyone thinks of her. I tell her she's crazy. Cathy says, "What's the big deal?" Do you know she's never been stalked by some psycho guy like you'd might expect? She's never experienced as much as an STD, rash, or even an awkward itch. Would I ever dare try something like that? I'm afraid I'd catch chlamydia just downloading the app.

Fear is a bully. It mocks me. It taunts me. It keeps me on the run. Running endlessly, cutting my feet on the shards of missed opportunities; spilling blood on the jagged edges of would-haves, should-haves, could-haves. Chasing me into the arms, and the body, of a man who is wrong. The wrong type. Wrong fit. The wrong everything . . . and I pray he doesn't leave me.

How would the story be different if I had risked it all and stood my ground with Abby Spencer? What if I had trusted that I would not meet an early death choking on the body of Christ? What if I had called fear's bluff instead of allowing fear to emerge victorious from countless confrontations without ever having to make a fist?

But what can I do?

All I can do, is do what I must.

DANIEL T BROWN

BLUE MOUNTAIN

I SAID yes! I said yes.

It had been my dream for the man I would marry to propose to me on Blue Mountain. My earliest memories were of me and my family singing along to the radio as we drove to our upstate cabin. The cabin had been in our family for generations. By the most scenic overlook on Blue Mountain Rest is where my father's father proposed to my grandmother. It's where my father promised my mother a lifetime of devotion in exchange for her hand in marriage.

I do give Jerry credit. I had mentioned my romantic connection to Blue Mountain during one of our first conversations, and apparently he was listening. We had even been to the cabin together several times over the last two years—birthday parties, parents' anniversaries, vacation getaways. So when we were heading home from a weekend trip and Jerry pulled into the overlook, my suspicions weren't raised at all.

He took my hand and led me to the road's edge to take in the green of the trees and the trickling of the lake below. That scenery never gets tired for me, and I was so in the moment that I didn't notice Jerry pulling the ring from his pocket.

I turned to find Jerry on one knee. The wind was whipping wild through the tree branches that day and causing a stir, but the words "will you marry me" came through clear as the sunlight.

And I said yes! Yes. Of course.

I remember my finger putting up little resistance as the diamond pushed over my knuckle and settled firm and snug. I'd never seen him so moved; tears were rolling down his cheeks into his beard. His arms pulled tightly around me, and in the most sincere voice he thanked me. Jerry thanked me for making this the happiest day of his life.

Returning the embrace, I thanked him for making my dream come true. But at the same time, I couldn't stop myself from thinking, If I pushed him off this cliff right then and there, would anyone ever find out?

Now I know that sounds kind of negative. Please, let me assure you that I have never seriously contemplated murdering anyone before. To me, it just seemed like a knee-jerk reaction to possibly making the biggest mistake of my life.

But you know it wouldn't be hard to make the whole thing look like some sort of accident. My family would be willing to swear on a hundred Bibles that I could never hurt anyone, let alone be a killer. And Jerry has crossed every member of his family. He only shows up for them when he wants money. So hell, they might even thank me if they found out I was responsible for his untimely demise.

I said yes. Why did I say yes?

It just so happens that I'm one of those people that hates to say no to anyone, and I honestly do love Jerry very much. If I had to rank him among all of my boyfriends, he'd be right there at the very top. I can't even think of a close second, and he's miles ahead of the guy who asked if I mind if he "shared me" with his cousins, or the wonderful gentleman who emailed my boss to say that I was a drug-dealing prostitute when I suggested that we consider seeing other people.

I never laughed so hard as I do when I am with Jerry. He has a way of making you feel like nothing or no one could ever get to you when he was at your side. However, there were signs I picked up along the way that told me that the "till death do us part" thing would not be without its challenges.

Like the time we had our baby scare. Over a course of a couple of days last summer, I thought that I was experiencing some of the signs of early pregnancy. I sit Jerry down to talk about it, and he jumps up and says, "What did you do?" What did "I" do, he says. It turned out to be nothing. But he went right to finger-pointing, and my heart sank. I'll never forget that.

A month ago I got a late-night call from my sister, whose daughter had just got hit by a car and needed emergency brain surgery. I booked a flight for the morning and hinted to Jerry that I could really use his company to deal with the stress. Jerry says that he "doesn't do hospitals very well" and decides that he would use the time that I was away to clean out his inbox. He said he didn't want to be in the way.

To marry Jerry I would have to understand that we would be partners during the good times, and I'd be flying solo when the real-life stuff went down.

As we stood at the Blue Mountain overlook, life seemed to shift into slow motion. I pulled my hands from around his back and set them against his chest. I would close my eyes, count to three and push.

At that moment reality kicked in and I realized that pushing Jerry from a cliff was a ridiculous idea and not the answer to my problem. The only rational thing to do was fake my own death, and start my life over down south. I'd change my name to Lily and sling hotcakes and root beer to truckers at a highway rest stop.

Maybe I'd meet a guy named Clint, or Hank, who wears a cowboy hat. He would take me out line dancing, and get into bar fights when other men hit on me.

Now it was all making sense.

Just then a powerful gust pushed me forward into Jerry's arms and he leaned in and kissed my lips with our bodies pressed tightly together. A warmth came over me and my heart raced. Jerry's kisses always let me know that there was a man in my life that loved me very much. His kiss always assured me that there was someone who accepted me and couldn't see all of my faults and flaws when they are so obvious to me.

Of course, it's miles from perfect. But when it's good, it's great. And when the bad shows up? We'll do what all mature, adult couples do— ignore it and pretend it doesn't exist.

After the kiss, Jerry looked me in the eyes, and said, "Do you mean it? You'll marry me?"

And I said yes.

TWELVE

A TWELVE-YEAR-OLD girl takes the stage.

This is the story of the day that Richard Esposito held my hand.

Richard Esposito. It was life changing. It was so real . . . and so unreal.

My first memory of Richard was when we started grade school together. In the early weeks of us all getting to know each other, some of the kids and even some teachers took to calling him Rich, or Richie. His mother found out and she sent him to school with a letter instructing everyone that they were to call him Richard. That was the name his parents chose for him. Ms. Mulgrew read it out loud in front of the whole class. He was so embarrassed.

Our families live on opposite ends of the channel. Over the years, me and Richard became friends. I was always impressed with what he knew about music and movies. He read books, and his family traveled. So he had experiences that fascinated me. Somewhere and sometime during sixth grade, he became a boy that I "liked." I began to find it hard not to be awkward and nerdy around him. I remember not being able to sleep the night he sent me a message saying that I was his best friend.

One afternoon our class was just settling back at our desks after being in the schoolyard when Mr. Angeles came in and said we were going back outside. "Put your coats on and make two lines in the hall," he said.

Now, normally when the classes lined up, one line was the girls and the other was the boys and we'd be in size order. I'd never be close to Richard. But this was different. There was no order to the lines, and Richard stood next to me. There was a lot of noise and confusion around us. It was getting loud, and I was starting to feel uncomfortable.

"Early dismissal and a three-day weekend," Richard muttered to me in an excited voice.
"Count me in," I said, joining in on his wishful thinking.

Then, out of nowhere, it happened. Richard reached over and put my hand in his. My heart jumped. I could feel it beating throughout my whole body. Richard looked at me. I looked at him. We both looked down at our hands joined together. Then we both looked away.

I remember thinking that this must be what love feels like. That when my parents say, "I love you," this is how they make each other feel. In love songs, or in romantic movies . . . this is what they're talking about.

Then, as quickly as you can blink your eyes, thoughts of love disappeared. Some of the seventh and eighth graders were running toward us from behind. It was like they were out of control. I asked Richard if he thought there was a fire.

Richard pulled me forward. He began to run and I ran to keep up. Our hands were still locked.

We went faster and faster, so fast that my winter hat flew from my head. I didn't look back. I raised my eyes to see Principal Lodow standing at the front door exit. She was waving us toward her and crying out for us all to run faster. She had tears in her eyes and a skinned-up knee from when she fell while rushing toward the door. Blood trickled and mixed with the scraped skin and torn stocking.

Eighth-grader Rene Howard was holding her little brother from first grade in her arms as she ran up beside us. That was the moment I found out what was actually happening.

"Gun" she yelled. "Campo's got a gun."

Richard and I made it out the door, and down the steps onto the front lawn. Students and faculty were everywhere. It was crazy. Police cars pulled up in front of the building. As the officers jumped out of their cars and ran toward the entrance, they were screaming for all of us to "Get down!" Richard and I fell onto the grass. Our hands separated.

I looked beside me and saw Richard lying with his head buried between his arms, which were folded in front of him. He was whimpering. He was terrified.

I wiped tears from my eyes and looked up at the front doors. I saw Mikey Campo from the fourth grade at the top of the stairs pointing a gun in the air and yelling something that I could not make out. The police surrounded Mikey and took the gun away. Then they carried him through the front plaza passed all of us. Mikey was kicking and fighting as he was put in the police car. When the police pulled away, we were all brought back into the school. Everyone's parents were called, and they came to get us.

On the news that night, they reported the story. Ten-year-old Michael Campo had brought a loaded gun to school. He had hidden it in the schoolyard days earlier and snuck it in after recess through the side door where there is no metal detector. It was his father's gun, and his father didn't even know the gun was missing. Mikey's parents kept him home from a Boy Scouts trip because of a bad report card. He brought the gun in and was threatening to shoot all the teachers for giving him low grades.

The part of the news story that stuck with me the most was when the reporter ended by saying, "Luckily, no one was injured." No one. I'd like to invite that reporter to come and visit us. I invite her to come and look in our eyes, feel what we feel, and tell me that no one was injured.

Come and visit the families that still haven't brought their kids back to school since that day and say that no one was injured.

I see Richard, but it's not the same. There's no talk about movies, or books and music. There's just an uncomfortable feeling. Maybe we remind each other too much of a day we'd both like to forget, and it's too hard. The story wasn't even on the front page of the newspapers. Another day, another gun in another school

The parent/student dance that had been scheduled two weeks after the incident was cancelled. Instead, we held a rally and wrote letters to our elected officials, asking them to do something. Do something to stop the guns. In return, they wrote back offering sympathy. Their hearts went out to us. They'll keep us in their thoughts and prayers

But thoughts and prayers won't keep us safe. Thoughts and prayers aren't bulletproof. Thoughts and prayers won't change the fact that the moment this twelve-year-old discovered love, it was forever ruined by the moment she discovered fear and terror.

I am twelve.
I am hurt.
I am angry.
I am confused.
I am scared.
I am twelve.

DANIEL T BROWN

MY EXPERIENCE WITH MARCUS

WHETHER or not Marcus was right when he pointed out that he and I had been riding the QM53 at the same time every day for close to a year and a half, I'm really not sure. But I took this friendly stranger at his word the wintery morning he first brought this observation to my attention. As we boarded the 7:20 bus, Marcus continued the conversation by politely introducing himself before taking the seat next to the one in which I had settled.

He said since it appeared that we were on the same journey, it only made sense that we at least know each other on a "hello" basis. I agreed. That became the onramp to a small-talk exchange between me and Marcus about the neighborhood, and how brutal Januarys can be for those of us who live so close to the ocean. When the momentum of our impersonal banter waned, Marcus opened up a bit by sharing stories of his travels with the wife and kids. He spoke of his growing distaste with the line of work he'd fallen into, and boasted of his dream of touring South America on a Harley Davidson Road King.

Among my contributions to the dialogue was telling the story of my trip to the Badlands of South Dakota with my boyfriend two years earlier. I still had some pics on my phone that I shared with Marcus of me at the Crazy Horse Monument, and us hanging out with the slew of bikers we ran into at a country music club in Sturgis. I finished the story, like I always do, by explaining how the relationship ended in front of Mount Rushmore during some stupid fight. Marcus and I laughed as I tried to describe the awkwardness of me and the man I once loved, but now hated, driving home in thirty hours of silence.

The next morning, and in the days moving forward, Marcus would be at the bus stop when I arrived. It became a regular thing for us to sit together for the ride into midtown Manhattan. One morning he saved my rear end when I was running late and the 53 was ready to pull away. Marcus stood at the bottom step of the bus and wouldn't let the driver close the door until I got on.

Most of our talk was just light stuff that helped pass the time on our commute. Once in a while things went a little deeper, like when Marcus asked me what my biggest fear was. He asked what I dreamed about as a child. One morning he asked if I had any regrets in life. If I could do anything over again, what would it be? I don't even remember answering a lot of those questions. Honestly, I preferred the small talk to those deeper inquiries, especially before my first cup of coffee.

My short and not-too-revealing answers were usually followed by Marcus carrying my end of the conversation with some revelations he discovered about himself during a long session of self-reflection. Even though I never felt like I brought a whole lot to the conversations, I appreciated when Marcus would tell me that I was interesting. Every now and then, he would go as far as to say that I was fascinating.

Marcus would also compliment me on being such a great listener. He appreciated how nonjudgmental I was. At one point Marcus confided that things weren't going so well at home. There was tension between him and his wife regarding plans and decisions about the future. I was saddened to learn this, and I extended myself as someone he could talk to.

I'm the last person to be giving relationship advice. I remember coughing up cliché responses such as, "Listen to your heart" and "Everyone has the right to be happy." To me, Marcus was a guy who needed to vent. He wasn't looking to me for answers. Marcus always thanked me for listening. Sometimes he would apologize for burdening me with his problems. I would say it's okay. I never saw it as a bother.

DANIEL T BROWN

Spring began to show its face, and the temperatures were on the rise. I had retired my winter coat to the back of the closet and put on my white denim jacket for the first time that morning. I was in high spirits, especially for a Monday, when we boarded the 7:20.

Marcus was in a good mood as well. We were barely a few blocks into the bus ride when he said that he had some news to tell me. Marcus went on to explain that he had thought at length about his present life. He had made the decision to leave his wife and seek a divorce. At this point, it was only a matter of Marcus choosing the proper moment to break the news of his impending departure to his family.

With me sitting beside him, Marcus removed the wedding ring from his finger and placed it in his inside jacket pocket. I was somewhat taken aback. Not only by his words, but by the manner in which he was describing such misfortune. The elation in Marcus' voice and look of joy in his eyes as he told the story of what sounded to me like devastating circumstances was difficult for me to wrap my head around.

Marcus paused and reached back into his pocket. He pulled out a thin chain, platinum gold. Attached was a gold heart outlined in small diamonds. Marcus said that he was originally going to buy the chain and heart for his wife. However, he never made the purchase due to the doubts that had taken root. Marcus said he preferred to save it for the woman he was truly meant for. It was his intention that the woman who wears these diamonds would never know the pain of a broken heart.

Marcus put a hand on my shoulder. "Thank you for helping me find my truth," he said while setting the chain into my open palm, which rested across my knee. I looked to the gold heart, and then up to Marcus. I felt the rush of the color running from my face. Simultaneously Marcus and I had a moment of clarity that left us speechless.

At once I came to the realization that, unbeknownst to me, Marcus and I had embarked on some kind of lovers' journey. At the same time,

Marcus discovered, to his great disappointment, that he and I were mere companions on a one-hour bus trip from Queens to Manhattan five days a week.

Not another word was exchanged between us. Pained by rejection, Marcus lifted the necklace from my palm, stood up, and walked to the backdoor of the bus. He exited at the next stop, though we were nowhere close to his destination. I sat paralyzed in silence for the remainder of the ride.

The following morning I arrived at the bus stop. Marcus was not there. A few moments before the 7:20 pulled in, I saw him walking in my direction. When he was within a few feet of where I stood, he pulled an envelope from his coat. He handed it to me. "Please read this," is all he said before turning back and walking away.

I was fearful, but not exactly sure why. Once I was seated for the commute, I debated opening what appeared to be a letter. Eventually, my curiosity took control, and I broke the envelope's seal and set my eyes upon the handwritten script on white notebook paper.

The letter began with an apology from Marcus for creating an uncomfortable situation for me on the bus the day before. From there Marcus expressed how he was confused by my "mixed signals." He couldn't understand how I could pull away from him after how I had encouraged him to leave his wife. He wrote that, in our very first conversation, I had agreed that we appeared to be "on the same journey."

He wrote that he knew for certain that we were meant to be together, and that, deep down, I knew it too. Marcus wrote that the thought of a life without me didn't seem like a life based on truth. Hearing me tell him that he had the right to be happy is what finally made him decide it was time to end things at home. In the letter, Marcus said that he was devastated that I wasn't more supportive when he broke the news that he was leaving his wife for me.

Marcus believed that, through engaging him in conversations about his thoughts and feelings, I had inspired him to dream. Because of me, he was going to abandon his present life, cash in, buy that Road King bike, and head for South America.

The letter ended with Marcus inviting me to accompany him. In two days' time, he would be waiting for me at the ferry dock at 108th Street. We would board that evening's last trip to Manhattan and figure things out from there. He wrote that a life together was our destiny. Marcus wrote that he believed that this was his truth.

I couldn't concentrate at work the entire day. I didn't sleep that night. I struggled to review every conversation between me and Marcus. Could I possibly have led him on? What signs did I miss? At what point did I become the other woman in his life?

I became depressed, then frightened. I cried. I got angry. I cycled through these emotions over the following forty-eight hours.

The thought that I would give up my life to run away with Marcus was absurd and completely out of touch with reality. I trashed the letter and tried to put the whole ordeal out of my mind. At the proposed moment intended for me to meet Marcus by the ferry landing to begin our life together, I was under my covers and wishing myself to sleep.

I never saw him again when boarding the 7:20 run of the QM53.

It may have been as much as a year later that I saw Marcus during a Saturday trip to a local farmers' market. He never saw me, but I observed from a distance as Marcus interacted with two children and the woman he had presented to me as his wife in photos during our bus conversations. He was wearing his wedding band.

There was laughter, joy, and the appearance of love and closeness among them. Though this was occurring at a comfortable distance from where

I stood, I wasn't too far away to notice the chain worn around the woman's neck, and the gold heart with diamonds that set against her chest between the open buttons of her collar. The chain that came with the promise that the one who wears it will never know the pain of a broken heart. Anger grew within me.

Did this woman have any idea that the man who gave her the gold heart, and the promise that came with it, had made that same promise to me? Was there any notion that the man she had sworn herself too, and whose vows for eternity she accepted, loved her with a wandering heart?

The temptation to approach her and open her eyes was pure, but I didn't.

Marcus spoke to me about truth. He would use the word like it meant something . . . like it meant everything. What does he know about truth?

And my truth? My truth is that I now find it difficult to welcome men into my life without internally questioning their motives. I watch my words. I'm careful when I speak. I do not receive compliments and encouragement from men in a positive way. I've been called out by male coworkers and acquaintances for presenting myself as guarded or overly protective of my personal space. The men who are picking up on these signals are reading me correctly.

I am no longer nonjudgmental. I am not a great listener. No one says that they find me fascinating. In the love relationships I've had since my experience with Marcus, I've ended things before they got too serious. Rather than feeling joy when a partner reveals that he loves me, I react with skepticism. With little provocation, I become insecure and jealous. When he takes too long to answer a call or text, I become fearful. When he's late, or our plans are changed, I wonder if I've been abandoned.

DANIEL T BROWN

Does he now view me as a mistake? Is he out in the world riding buses, falling in love with strangers, and telling them how I've failed him? I'm no longer his truth. Is his secret love watching from a distance as I carry on with him under the false belief that his commitment to me is real?

Please. If you're thinking of rolling your eyes at me like I've completely lost my grip, I'm warning you not to. If you think that I'm the one with the attitude issue, you'd be doing yourself a great service by keeping it to yourself. If you're dying to ask me what the hell my problem is, do it at your own risk. Because I'll go right for your throat.

And that right there, on this day and at this moment, is me living my truth.

NIGHT OF THE FLAT-CHESTED

IN my high school years, I used to lie awake and dream of being beautiful and popular. My best friends in 1979 were Tammy Louis and Maria Pesta. Together, we were invisible in the halls and classrooms. I guess that's not entirely true. The jocks did see us and even liked to refer to us as the "straight A students." However, that had more to do with our cup sizes than our grades.

In the opening semester of sophomore year, we found ourselves in Ms. Riverton's gym class. It was apparent to her that we were outcasts, and she went easy on us. That same fall, rumors started going around about Ms. Riverton. From what we heard, she had brought a female partner to a retreat that some of the teachers had organized upstate on a summer break. It wasn't even a Board of Ed event.

When the rumors began reaching the parents, the principal started getting complaints about Ms. Riverton's "lifestyle." There was a private meeting with the school administration and PTA. Ms. Riverton was told that the school wasn't looking to make trouble for her. She could keep her job under the condition that she will not speak about her personal life with students or bring female companions to any school or Board of Ed events.

She refused. Elizabeth Riverton refused to deny, ignore, or take on any of the world's bullshit guilt and shame over who she was. Instead, she began bringing her partner to the school dances, rallies, and fundraisers. Things got nasty.

Some of the parents actually believed that Ms. Riverton's "gayness" might rub off on us and turn us into homosexuals. One parent even said out loud at a meeting, "What she does in her own home is her business. But why does she have to bring it out into the world?" That parent was my own mother.

I remember attending one of the neighborhood protests where community members were speaking out against Ms. Riverton teaching in our school. Elizabeth attended as well and asked to speak.

She addressed the angry room and explained that she loved being a teacher. She was proud to play a role in the shaping of young minds. She then began telling a story about growing up in Jackson Heights in the period where the ink on the Civil Rights Act was still fresh only fifteen years earlier. At dinner, her parents would discuss the tenants' meetings at her apartment complex, where longtime residents raised questions like "What are we going to do about these animals that want to move in?"

One night, a group of Elizabeth's neighbors came to visit her parents and asked if they would join them in a protest to stop the building management from allowing nonwhites to rent from the complex. "Nonwhites" wasn't exactly the word they used. Ms. Riverton's parents would not participate. They lost friends. They got harassed.

Elizabeth Riverton assured the room that nothing she was teaching the students was leading them toward homosexuality. And then she asked what we were teaching young people by asking those around them to feel shame for being who they are.

Some parents circulated a petition that night to call on the principal to no longer allow Ms. Riverton access to the girls' locker room. They feared for their daughters' safety. Three hundred parents signed it, mine included. I didn't speak with them for weeks. The principal caved and succumbed to the demands of the petition

If I told you that there was barely a lick of self-esteem among me, Tammy, and Maria combined back then, it's no exaggeration. But seeing a person who reached out and took an interest in our lives be publicly devastated and humiliated was beyond what we could handle.

The problem was that we were going up against large numbers. They had the administration and all the power. No matter what plan we devised, the truth was clear that we could only get this done by getting the student body on our side. The jocks, the pretty girls, the rockers and disco kids, punks, and geeks. We fit in with none of them, and we needed to appeal to them all.

Each year on the first Thursday evening in November, the student government hosted a formal dinner dance to raise money for a community Thanksgiving turkey giveaway. The event always took place at the American Legion Hall, and some of the students would perform skits or songs, and announce the donations as they came in.

The plan was for Maria, Tammy, and I to ask for a moment to speak and address the room. The ruse was that we'd speak on setting up a volunteer database to give out turkeys, but we would seize the moment and talk about what had been done to Ms. Riverton. We would call on every student to walk out of the school the next day after homeroom.

The three of us were scared to death while waiting for our opportunity to speak. As bad luck would have it, we would be following a presentation to the homecoming king and queen, Mark Lester, the football team quarterback, and his girlfriend, Tricia Ottson. Tricia was destined for Ivy League college life and also happened to be the president of the "I'm way too smart and hot to talk to you, stick up my ass" club.

Mark got on the mic, asked the DJ to stop playing, and read our introduction. "And now, we have an important message from Alice Mather, Tammy Louis, and Maria Pesta." It was dead quiet. I held the short speech that we worked on together, and I stepped to the mic. I began to speak, but could barely get out more than a whisper. Mark grabbed the speech out of my hand and took the mic.

He read out loud in a booming voice in front of everyone about how the three of us were offended and how shaming Ms. Riverton was a disgrace. Many of the students, as well as the parents and faculty, laughed as Mark announced that Alice, Maria, and Tammy were calling on the students to fight back and walk out of school the next day.

Mark lowered the notes from in front of his face. He looked at us and then to the crowd. "Well, look what we have here," he said as I felt my forehead and hands getting sweaty. "Rebel nerds," Mark called us as the room erupted in laughter. "Or maybe we should call them rebels without a date," Mark continued to work the room.

With the crowd in his hand, he went for the kill. "Maybe someday, they'll make a movie of this night and they can call it *Night of the Flat-Chested.*"

I was dying inside. I looked up to see the principal heading up the steps of the stage to stop the bludgeoning. I felt faint. Then something very strange happened.

"Hold on a second." Mark pointed at the principal on stage. "These girls want a walkout." Again, the room was silent. "Ms. Riverton has always been cool with us. What's up with giving her a hard time?"

"I say we do it. Let's go for it!"

The students were tipsy on rebellion and filled the room with applause. With that, the principal's jaw dropped. A chant began to drown out all other sound, "Walk out, walk out . . . walk out."

Sure enough, on a breezy Friday morning at 9:30 a.m., students walked out to protest the banning of Ms. Elizabeth Riverton from the girls' locker room. We brought some homemade protest signs and people held them.

We filled the plaza at the school steps and the protest poured into the street. I'm not sure how word got out, but newspaper reporters and TV news vans showed up.

By the following week, there was a reversal, and Ms. Riverton was allowed access to any facility in which other female teachers had access. She was also permitted to bring her partner to school events where faculty significant others were invited. She got an apology.

When Hurricane Sandy hit in October 2012, the school's soccer field was destroyed. I immediately got ahold of Maria and Tammy. We're still friends today. We began reaching out to every elected official and school alum that we could find. Our petition called on the city to name the rebuilt facility Elizabeth Riverton Field. We testified before the city council. Tammy brought her kids, and they testified together. Some of the students from back then came forth to testify as well. My parents came and spoke in favor of the field naming.

In the spring of 2015, construction broke ground on Elizabeth Riverton Field. There was a ceremony for the groundbreaking. Ms. Riverton had moved to Colorado some years earlier, but through the magic of Facebook, we found her and she came.

When it was Elizabeth's turn to speak at the ceremony, she was moved to tears. She was overwhelmed. Elizabeth finished her remarks by reminding us all that just as in the sixties, our protest in the seventies, and as we celebrated together that day, the fight for the freedom of one is the fight for freedom for all. To tell one of us to get in line is to insist that we all get in line. A demand for one of us to conform is the demand that we all conform.

As for the rebel nerds, standing up for what was right didn't make our boobs any bigger or our eyes any bluer. It didn't help our SAT scores or raise our grades. But standing up and speaking up put us on the right side of history in our tiny little part of the world. And thirty-four years later, Alice Mather, Tammy Lois, and Maria Pesta were the most popular kids in the graduating class of 1981.

MY BRAIN IS IN A BLENDER

THE periods when my mind and my feet are together in the same room simultaneously are becoming fewer and farther between. For people like me of a certain age and station, the inability to live in the present is dismissed as normal . . . described as "brain freeze," some kind of deficit disorder, or merely "senior moments." But I dare say that something more insidious is afoot.

It is in my heart that I believe that the longer I participate in the human experience, the more my attention and focus vehemently reject the here and now.

I find that I'm mostly present for the beginnings and endings of person-to-person exchanges. As far as what takes place between "Hi. How are you?" and "See you later," my presence is solely physical.

Distraction reveals itself to me. I'm invited to join on an adventure into the part of me that is dark. I am willing to explore.

There's a commotion up ahead, and soon I'm being asked to take sides in the street fight between what I'm striving to be and the acceptance that what I am at this moment is good enough.

My brain is in a blender, a transporter time machine fueled by the anxiety that comes with the fear of not knowing. The future . . . it's cold, and the language is foreign.

I'll be left without enough. I know it.

I will be alone. Of this I am certain.

Who will love me when the beauty has left my body? Who will find me when death stakes its claim? No one. I am sure.

Nearby is the garden where the phobias and apprehensions grow mighty. Where no amount of prayer and chemistry mixed into the soil can slow the harvest.

I affirm the positive mantra, but the revolt is weak and shouted down. As if any attempts at comfort can unring the bell of knowing that I'm just one missed paycheck, one flood, one fire, one spot on an X-ray away from my entire house of cards caving in.

And then what? What happens then?

Turning, I notice that I have been left stranded, so I retrace my steps along the tightly wound road to the immediate and current. My inbox, Excel sheets, the whims of my superiors, the new high score in that mindless game, that second season, those comments that require my response.

From now on, I will try harder. I will do better. I will listen and follow the instructions. One step, one moment, one day at a time.

What was I just saying? What's that story you were telling me? I'm sorry. Worry is my master, and I must obey when called.

For some of us, the present is a luxury. I have found that the rent for living in the now is much more than I can afford.

I hear tomorrow's footsteps. It's terrifying. Of that, I am positive.

DANIEL T BROWN

SIX MINUTES TO LIFE

W HAT is your very first memory?

Could you possibly remember your first steps? What was the first sound you made . . . the first word you learned?

How about your first knee scrape, bad dream, birthday party, sitting on Santa's lap?

When was the first time you cried so hard that you were beyond being consoled, or the first time something made you laugh so hard that you fought to catch your breath?

Do you remember being carried on your father's shoulders? You were as high as the clouds, but you felt safe and protected . . . like you were on top of the world.

Have you ever felt that secure again?

Can you think back to when you held your mother's hand, walking to that first day of school? Were you excited? Maybe frightened? Were you a future teacher's pet, a troublemaker, or did you just blend in?

Wasn't it you that was standing in the schoolyard wanting to be accepted and liked by the cool kids so much that you were willing to do anything, or tell any lie to get yourself in? Later, when you discovered that it wasn't worth it, you promised yourself that you would never again sell your soul to get someone to like you. Of course, that turned out to be the biggest lie of all.

Who was that first crush? Remember what it felt like the first time your heart was stolen by someone who didn't even know you existed?

Can anything match the joy of seeing the pride in your parents' eyes as you accepted that diploma on graduation day? You felt all grown up and childlike at the same moment.

Do you remember how much courage it took to put your entire heart and soul on the line when you told that one person that you were meant for that you loved them, hoping with every fiber of your soul that you would hear them say it back?

How proud were you to stand beside your family, your friends, and your God, and state your devotion and lifelong commitment to that one person that was put on earth just for you?

Remember the vows you wrote and the weightless bliss of handing your heart to someone else and pledging them eternity?

How soon were you ready to take it all back when he left the damn toilet seat up for the hundredth time, or when he forgot about your birthday? How about when she threw out that perfectly good T-shirt that smells like sour milk, the one you've only been wearing since 1991?

It's the powerful love of life; the joy of taking air in your lungs and knowing that there were no limits to what you could be or do!

It's walking down the street at Christmastime and the lights and music take your breath away. People are smiling, happy, and bright with holiday spirit. All you can see is the very best in humanity. You see love and kindness, and you suddenly find yourself getting angry at those who are offended when people use the word "Christmas." You're overcome with the urge to stand in the middle of the street, stop traffic, and yell, "Let's not take the Christ out of Christmas!"

Then you remember that you're Jewish and the issue is none of your business. You're reminded of what your therapist said about your need to take on other people's problems and make them your own.

Did you almost pass out the day you learned that you would soon be giving birth to a brand-new human being? Have you ever experienced that much elation and fear at the same time?

It's the moment you hold your precious baby in your arms and you turn to your partner and say, "Dear God, look what we've created."

It's the moment fifteen years later when you're called to the police precinct because that precious child got drunk and arrested for breaking and entering . . . again . . . and you turn to your partner and say, "Dear God, look what we've created."

Will you ever forget how your heart sank when your teenager broke curfew and your countless calls went to voice mail? You didn't want to overact and call the police, but every minute felt like an eternity, and the pain and fear twisted in your gut like a jagged knife. Then he walked through the door with that "what's the big deal" look on his face that always makes you see red. You hugged him, thanked God, and promised him that the next time he pulls something like that will be the last time.

Do you remember how surprised you were at yourself the first time you felt lust for someone and forgot for a brief moment that you were promised to someone else?

Do you remember how surprised you were at yourself the first time you felt lust for someone and forgot for a brief moment that you were promised to someone else, then allowed yourself to forget again?

How deep was the heartbreak when you released your frail mother's hand and said goodbye as her breathing grew lower than a whisper before her heart stopped beating?

How about the first time someone younger than you dies of old age?

Did you find religion again the day the doctor called to say that something showed up on your blood test and you needed to come in for a second look? The doctor said there was nothing to worry about yet. However, for you, there was plenty to worry about.

It's looking back on your life story. What do you regret? How much do you wish you could do over? Are you satisfied?

You shut your eyes and say your prayers.

Your last laugh, last tear, last smile, last touch . . . last breath.

MR. 5:15

ABOUT nine months ago, it was suggested, strongly, that I return to psychotherapy. Hey, no problem.

Since the sessions began, I'd maintained the Wednesday 6:00 pm appointment. That spot is mine. Sometimes, there would be a need for more than one session in a week, but the six o'clock Wednesday slot is the constant.

The rub of my having a steady appointment is that the patient that has the 5:15, the appointment right before mine, has also been the same person for these nine months.

This means that when our therapist opens her office door each week at six and I'm in the waiting room, me and Mr. 5:15 are forced to walk past each other. I'm entering the office as he's leaving.

Mr. 5:15 and I have this unspoken agreement not to make eye contact during the exchange. Still, curiosity forces us both to steal a glance of the other. As we pass, I do my best to raise my shoulders, suck in my stomach, and maintain a sane and healthy posture. Mr. 5:15 makes a few temporary adjustments as well, and we both try not to look too mentally unstable in front of each other.

Every Wednesday at six o'clock, the office door opens and Sheila Miller, PsyD says goodbye to him before saying, "Come on in, Cindy." And that's something that really gets under my skin. How come Mr. 5:15 gets to know my name, but I don't get to know his?

After a few months of that bullshit, I finally got the nerve to call Sheila Miller, PsyD out on this. I suggested that, instead of using my real name, we come up with an alias for me that we could use when it was time for me to enter her office. I brought in a list of possible fake names. I preferred Phoebe. However, Dr. Sheila Miller thought that the better solution was for her to just stop saying my name rather than go with my perfectly good alias idea during the appointment switch. Whatever.

Then I made my case that since Mr. 5:15 already got to know my name, it was only fair that I got to know his. Sheila Miller, PsyD shot that idea down as well. She said that this was unethical and that she wasn't comfortable giving me the name of a fellow client. I pointed out how she seemed to be pretty comfortable outing me, and that ethics and morals didn't seem to be an issue until it was time to level the playing field.

Sheila Miller then did that thing she does and accused me of creating "growth obstacles" in our work together. She asked me to consider whether I am stirring up these controversies as my way of keeping us from talking about what's really going on with me. It's a trick that she pulls whenever I catch her working against me.

She pulls the same nonsense whenever I complain that she needs to be doing something about the brothel that operates across from the G train station by her office. The illicit operation runs under the name of the Nu-Age Wellness Spa. However, any fool can see that the only "wellness" going on under this roof is allowing men to come and cheat on their wives by indulging in illegal, not to mention immoral, sex acts.

Sheila Miller said I have no proof that the Nu-Age Wellness Spa is a whorehouse, so she refused to take me seriously about the matter.

I was determined to prove to Sheila Miller that there was wrongdoing going on at this place. Then one day, all the proof that I needed fell right into my lap. It was just another Wednesday evening when I was headed back to the G train after a session. I'm walking by the Nu-Age

Wellness Spa and who do I see coming out? Mr. 5:15. And get this, as he's turning out of the whorehouse doorway, he sees me approaching up the block. This time, I'm looking right at him with my best "let's see you explain your way out of this" stare.

Mr. 5:15 doesn't even acknowledge me. He just walks by me like nothing's wrong.

Well, you better believe that I marched right back to the office of one Sheila Miller, PsyD. I couldn't wait to see her face when I told her what Mr. 5:15, Mr. Wonderful whose name we dare not speak, is doing with his evenings. By the time I got to the office, I see Sheila Miller exiting the building.

I come running up and I lay it all out there for her . . . in graphic detail, but she could not care less. She says that by keeping tabs on her other clients, I'm putting her in a very awkward spot. Again, she completely takes his side.

That's the thanks I get. After bringing to her attention that I can swear with full certainty that I'm 90 percent . . . at least 80 to 90 percent sure that one of her clients is a certified sex offender, Sheila Miller, PsyD says it's all fine and dandy with her.

Tell me. Be honest. Is it me?

Sheila Miller PsyD says that I would not be experiencing so many of these negative thoughts and paranoid episodes if I would just go back on my medication, like pills are the answer to everything. That's the exact same wonderful advice that my ex had for me when I got wise on his perverted leanings.

Everything appeared to be going along okay with him, then out of nowhere, we hit a bad spot with his ability to make himself available to me intimately. He's uncomfortable making love to me while my "symptoms are going untreated." Yeah . . . all right. I'll play along.

One day, I came across him sitting on the sofa going through a Lands' End catalog. I took a peek and I saw that he's checking out the women's feet in the shoe section. Quickly, he turned the page when he saw that I'd busted him.

But I didn't confront him. Not yet. But then he got sloppy. Twice I find the catalog left open to the exact same page. Once I found the catalog in his briefcase during a routine search of his personal belongings. The second time, I saw it in the drawer of his nightstand by our bed.

It was around the holidays, so that evening, we were setting up the Christmas tree and getting all into the spirit. He's still acting like everything's normal and he's not some kind of foot-licking psycho. I couldn't take it anymore. So I went into the bedroom and grabbed the catalog, the one that he's turned into his own little porn magazine, and I confronted the pig.

Like every other deviant, he started his whole denial routine. But I'm not having it. Not on my watch. He started acting all hurt like he's the victim. He said I spoiled his "surprise." He said that the reason he had been looking at that page is because I had pointed those shoes out to him and said I really liked them. Yes, I had told him how I wanted the shoes, but not for one minute am I going to let him turn this whole thing around on me.

Next thing I know, he's pulling a box out of the closet. It's all gift wrapped with a bow and the whole nine. I'm told to open it, and guess what? The same shoes from the page are in the box. He said it's a present for me. He said that he was so looking forward to giving me the shoes on Christmas morning, but now I've ruined everything with a crazy accusation.

DANIEL T BROWN

And he's saying all of this with a straight face. Daniel Day Lewis couldn't have done a better acting job. I tell him that the lies stop right now. I said, "Get the F-U-C-K out of my home." For the sake of full disclosure, it was actually his apartment, so I was the one who had to leave. But my point was made.

He was another one pushing me to take pills, so I won't feel. You know, so I won't notice that I'm being played and screwed over. Everyone's answer is for me to swallow a pill and all of the bad will go away.

Sheila Miller asked me how I can possibly expect to adjust and maintain a healthy existence if I continue to make the same mistakes over and over.

She called me before our next session to tell me that she will only continue to see me under the condition that discussions about Mr. 5:15 or any other of her clients were, from now on, off limits.

Okay, Sheila Miller, PsyD, whatever you say.

When that next Wednesday at six o'clock arrived, the door opened and Mr. 5:15 and I crossed paths. I walked by with a look on my face that let the world know that it was all good.

Maybe halfway into my session, I acted like I was getting a call on my cell. I acted all concerned, and then I told Sheila Miller that it's an emergency and I have to run. I rushed out of the office and headed toward the G train, but I'm not going to the train station. I stormed right up to the Nu-Age Wellness Spa. I'm thinking, if Sheila Miller, PsyD wants proof, it's proof she shall have.

I made a quick call before storming my way into the whorehouse for a showdown with Mr. 5:15 that is long overdue.

I got in there and saw a group of ladies pretending to be giving manicures, pedis, and skin treatments. I started calling out, "Where are the whores?" but these sex workers are well trained and they started giving me looks like "What's this lady's problem?"

The madam of the place walked up to me and said that if I don't leave, she was calling the police. But I immediately flipped the script and let her know that I've already called the police and they would be joining us at any minute to shut down this den of iniquity.

By the time the cops showed up, I was in the backroom turning the place inside out looking for Mr. 5:15 to show himself. But he didn't have the stones to face me.

If I had any idea as to what was going to happen next, I probably would've had second thoughts about launching the raid. The officers that answered my call to the Nu-Age Wellness Spa weren't interested in taking down hookers or pulling Mr. 5:15 out of whatever dark corner he was hiding in.

Instead, I was the one placed in restraints and being advised of my rights. In a world where everyone else has the right to act depraved and fornicate freely without care or conscience, all that was left for me was the right to remain silent.

I wasn't thrilled about being moved back into my room at the hospital. Sometimes, I think that for me, all roads lead to the bed, three meals, and soft, slip-on shoes at the ward. And the pills. Back to the pills.

Sheila Miller, PsyD came to visit. She wanted to know why I never follow the plan when I get released. She wondered why I continue to choose not to get better.

I asked why do I have to get better when every time I meet the world, things only get worse. I'm confined to the space between four walls, and the sick, bad people live freely.

No pills. No soft, slip-on shoes for the whores, the nameless men who degrade women, or the boys who hold back their love . . . and say it's all my fault. No growth obstacle accusations for Sheila Miller when she lies, keeps secrets, or silences me when I say it's all wrong.

I'll play along . . . for now. But when I'm out again . . . and I will find my way out, I'll let everyone know the truth. But look at you all now. You don't get it. You don't see it. Maybe they've gotten to you and you're all on pills. You can't feel it. You can't see.

But I'll be back. And you'll all learn the truth.

You have no idea. No idea at all.

THE LESSON

I DON'T remember if there was ever a time in my childhood when becoming a teacher wasn't my ambition. Throughout my years in school, I always looked up to my teachers. As a teenager, I would fantasize about leading a classroom of students through a lesson plan I'd created. I'd literally get goosebumps. I couldn't imagine a greater contribution that one person could make to society than to play a role in the shaping and educating of future generations.

Early on in my teaching career, I discovered that I connected best with students at the high school level. I'd often been viewed as approachable. Teens navigating through the challenges of their high school years frequently saw me as someone they could bring their problems to and bounce ideas off. There were few students that I connected with as strongly as Emily Ford. She had been in my literature classes through her sophomore, junior, and senior years. I "got" Emily. I really did. She saw that.

Emily was someone I would describe as a "life liver." She wanted to learn and experience everything. Aside from being a star in academics, Emily was a burgeoning artist: a painter who captured the world on canvas brilliantly, with a unique and personal perspective. It's so rare to see that in the art of someone her age.

An issue that Emily had been putting off for some time was breaking the news to her parents that she was not planning on attending college after graduation. Instead, Emily wanted to tour the landscapes of Ireland, Italy, and South Africa. She wanted to experience cultures and develop further as an artist. By this point, painting had become her passion.

However, Emily's parents had been making plans for her Ivy League college and grad school career well before she was born. Her mother and father had each earned multiple master's degrees and had forged very successful careers in their chosen fields. The news that Emily had no interest in higher learning was not something her parents were going to accept without raising holy hell.

It was being able to speak with a student like Emily about issues such as this that fueled my exuberance to go to work each day. I truly believed that Emily owed it to herself to follow her own heart and pursue the future that she planned. Though Emily had the choice of a couple of highly ranked schools, I was convinced that for her to attend college only because she was afraid to go against her parents' wishes was something she would regret.

I encouraged Emily to sit her parents down and let them know how she felt. As Emily would be eighteen by the time the fall semester was to start, I reminded her that she would be a legal adult. The choice was really hers alone to make.

Well, by the next afternoon, I had Emily's parents in my classroom and way up in my face. They wanted to know who I thought I was to be giving their daughter such reckless and irresponsible advice.

I told them that Emily had a gift. There was an unlimited potential within Emily that needed to be recognized. I said that we should support her decision to see the world and create art. Emily had a dream. Why not let her pursue it?

My well-intended offering was rejected as if it were poisonous.

"Do you have any idea how immature and foolish you sound?" Lily's mother unloaded on me before they exited the classroom. Their next stop was to see the principal to make a formal complaint about me.

The school's principal was Denise DeMolea, a very bright and progressive woman about ten years my senior. She was my superior, as well as someone I'd come to recognize as a friend. It was beyond demoralizing to stand before Denise as she reprimanded me for what she described as "unprofessional" and "careless" behavior.

Being attorneys, Emily's parents threatened lawsuits. For the "unprofessional" act of encouraging a young person to be true to herself, I was suspended from my job. Fearing that I might lose my teaching certification, I agreed to a transfer.

I started over in a school in a neighboring district. It's a middle school. Not my first choice, but what can you do? Never again have I allowed myself to get personally or emotionally involved in the lives of my students. Teaching has become more of a job for me. No longer is it my life. It's now my livelihood. I stay out of trouble. I stay professional.

Years later, Emily's senior class had a reunion. A few of my friends from the faculty back then invited me to come. I was hoping to see Emily at the event, and our paths did cross.

She had spent the better part of four years abroad after graduating high school trying to make her way as a painter. Eventually, she was no longer able to sustain the existence of an artist. Emily returned and was ready to go the nine-to-five route. The Ivy League was no longer an option for her. At the time of our conversation, Emily was making a living teaching art in a community center after-school program. She also had an adjunct position teaching continuing education courses with the city university.

What was most noticeable to me about Emily is that she seemed happy and content with herself.

I told her that I was sorry about my handling of things back when she was my student. When I expressed my regrets, Emily wondered why I felt the need to apologize.

Emily said that if she ever had to counsel a student on whether to choose between a sure thing and security for their future, or follow the uncertain path of pursuing their passion, she would tell that person to chase their dream. No doubt about it.

All I could offer Emily for a response was a smile that communicated politeness. Inside, I couldn't keep myself from thinking about how immature and foolish she sounded.

OURSELVES

I N this moment, I ask that you allow yourself to imagine that heaven exists right here on earth, and we all live in heaven together. Here, anything and everything is possible.

Picture in your mind that in heaven, we are free. We are free to live and love, and we all have every opportunity to be whoever we dream to be. Class and status are fluid. The meek can be mighty, and everybody is somebody.

Know it in your heart that in this earthly heaven, it is simply understood that these are the blessings bestowed upon each of us. Once upon a time, these were promises made. These are our rights. And these freedoms, rights, and dreams exist for everyone . . . everyone but you.

But because there is so much for so many to be grateful for, the majority becomes cross that everyone doesn't share in the gratitude. The majority believes that you would be afforded all the same benefits and opportunities as them if you would just make the small concession of denying who you really are. Could you please just conform and be something that doesn't make others uncomfortable?

They preach conformity until your unwillingness to see it their way makes them angry. Eventually, that anger turns to hate. The hatred gets so intense that they are willing to literally murder you. And if they can't kill you, they push you to the point where you're ready to take your own life.

One person's fairy tale is another's tragedy.

Just be yourself—how often have we heard that pearl of wisdom being doled out as heartfelt advice? Two things I know for sure: the person who first suggested to someone that everything would be all right if they just be themselves was a white man. Secondly, he certainly was not offering that advice to a woman with a penis.

In the first moments of my life, I was declared a boy. This determination was made by a doctor based on the belief that the anatomy I presented met the accepted definition of male. Unfortunately, I was not consulted on this matter. For if I was, I would have surely set the record straight.

I'd have to believe that even if I had emerged from the womb with the power to debate my gender, I still would have been overruled by a doctor, my parents, and an entire society who would have pointed between my legs and rested their case.

Of course, when I refer to the fairy-tale land, I'm speaking of America. Please know that even with the challenges and outright abuse I've encountered for being an "unconventional woman" in America, from the bottom of my heart, I believe that my country is the closest thing to heaven on earth.

My story does not include brutal beatings. I've never been assaulted on any serious level, and the only death threat I've ever witnessed was from a Macy's cosmetics counter salesgirl who told me she'd kill to have my eyebrows.

What eventually broke me was the accumulation of unrelenting and exhausting stares, judgment, ridicule, and all-out rejection hurled my way from those I was supposed to live side by side with in this earthly paradise.

Reliving over and over experiences such as going to a job interview and seeing that look on the employer's face when they get that first view of me. The look that says "no fucking way can I hire you."

How many eye rolls and smirks from judgmental spectators have I ignored? How many tears have I fought to hold back when hateful, vulgar words are said to my face without a hint of remorse? Why do you continue to call me sir when I've corrected you a thousand times?

What about the time that a group of drunk assholes on the A train dared the weakest of their bunch to grab my ass? They laughed, and I laughed too. I pretended to think that it was funny. On the inside, I was terrified that if I revealed my anger, they would jump me and nobody would call for help.

It's always something. Every damn day.

Meanwhile, kids are killing kids every day with guns that are so easily made available. Each day, the planet becomes less inhabitable, as the sea levels rise and the oceans creep to our doorsteps. Yet, we close our eyes. Apparently, the only time anyone is ready to get off the couch and take a stand is when I make my way toward the door of the ladies' room.

It all got so loud. Hate . . . it's deafening. I was willing to entertain any means necessary to drown it all out. I turned to the needle, and the needle brought relief.

The night I surrendered and set out to make my transition from the living to the dearly departed, I blasted the ripest vein in my left arm with what I would later learn was enough heroin to kill three people my size.

It was so peaceful. The calm and quiet claimed me. My escape was imminent.

I came to on a gurney in an ambulance, rushing toward the medical team that would pull me from the grave that I had dug myself. During the ride, my nearly lifeless hand was held in the grip of a man I knew simply as Floyd. Up until that moment, Floyd was only known to me as the friendly porter in my apartment building.

Our paths would cross on occasion and greetings exchanged. However, Floyd discovered my dying body sprawled across my doorway and he believed that my life was worth saving. That intervention also put Floyd and me on a pathway toward what has become a deep connection.

What bonds Floyd and me is not a bloodline, a shared gender, ethnicity, or culture. The link simply rests in the fact that as a black man of a certain age, Floyd's exterior earned him a map to the American Dream that simply read "You can't get there from here."

As a high school student in the late 1960s, Floyd spoke with his grade counselor of his ambition to attend college. He asked the counselor if there were any extracurricular programs that he could be enrolled in to bring up his grades in order to get into a good university.

The following evening, there was a knock at his door. His parents answered to find the high school basketball coach on their porch. The coach had come by to recruit Floyd for the team at the counselor's request. The counselor believed that Floyd's only opportunity, being a black kid, for college was through athletics. The person who was supposed to be Floyd's mentor never considered that a young black man had the potential to make it to a good college through academics.

Possessing no real athletic ability, Floyd didn't make the team. Frustrated with the entire process, he dropped out of high school at seventeen. And though his country saw the color of his skin as a disability that burned the bridge to his dreams, that same country saw him fit and able enough to defend the very rights and freedom he was denied on the battlefield of Vietnam.

During a visit to my rehab, I asked Floyd where he puts the anger. He said, "When they control your world, that's a sin on them. But when you let them control your mind, that sin is on you." Floyd taught me that rather than cursing God for the way things are, I should thank God. I should thank God for the pain because that pain will help others. When someone tells me that they have been a victim of hate, I can say I know . . . I know how it feels. When I cross paths with others who put themselves at risk just for daring to be who they are, I can tell them that I've been there . . . and I'm still here.

Floyd taught me to dream again. He taught me to imagine. Imagine a day when we all live in paradise together. And in this paradise, a paradise known as America, it is okay for all of us to just be ourselves.

Imagine that here is where a "happily ever after" is a possibility for everyone. Imagine that the American Dream is more than just a fairy tale. Imagine that freedom, real freedom, is more than just our founding fathers' greatest work of fiction.

Imagine that.

BAD, BAD WOLF

YOU'RE a heartbreaking, no-good wolf of a guy
  Licking those lips when you give me the eye
 Laying it on thick with the lies that I'm believing
And those great, big eyes that are all the better for deceiving

Get back
Get back

Bad wolf boy plays a girl for a fool
Got my heart on a string, and he's playing it cool
I know that you're cheating when you say that you'll be true
Grandma always warned me about a wolf like you

Get back
Get back
You better get back to the wolf pack

Get back
Get back

You better get back to the wolf pack
'Cause this red ridin' hood has caught you with the goods
So you better get back to the woods.

You got a line for the ladies, come off sweet as can be
Never should have let you get your claws into me
You bring me red roses that will make a girl swoon
And a kiss on the lips that makes me howl at the moon

Get back
Get back

Like the breeze through the trees, you got me weak in the knees
When I'm skipping along the trail

It's my tough wolf lover waiting underneath the covers
It's a bad, bad fairy tale
Oh get back!

I'm a sucker for your badness, what can I say
My heart beats faster when you push me away
Drives me crazy when you're acting so tough
You're a bad, bad wolf, and I can't get enough

Get back
Get back
You better get back to the wolf pack

Get back
Get back

You better get back to the wolf pack
'Cause this red ridin' hood has caught you with the goods
So you better get back to the woods

ALL OF THE ABOVE

I F you were lucky enough to have known my father, you would agree that he was a vibrant and brilliant human being. The man was filled with love. He was tough and strong, an air force veteran of the Korean War who was doing his own house repairs and tree pruning well into his later years. It would put such a scare in me when I'd find my father by himself high on a ladder or climbing onto our roof with a tool belt around his waist. I'd yell up at him, "Are you crazy, deranged, or just a plain old fool?"

My dad's comeback would always be, "If you're asking me, I'm going to have to go with all of the above."

Not long after his eighty-fourth birthday, my father developed a heart condition. Along with multiple medications, the illness forced him to carry a heart monitor with a sensor and battery that he wore over his shoulder with a strap. The contraption hung by his waist outside of his clothes. It was equally intrusive and unsightly. The device dramatically limited his ability to work. He saw the battery as a bulky, crude reminder of his advanced age and frailty. Additionally, when his forgetfulness and growing loss of control over basic bodily functions further robbed this very proud man of his dignity, my father made a decision.

The choice to end his life rather than deteriorate to the point of incapacitation was not motivated by pride, stubbornness, or even self-pity. The decision was rooted in a belief. Above all else, my father was a deeply religious man who devoted himself to living by commandments, parables, and an unwavering devotion to the risen Christ. The decision to terminate his life was simply the act of a man welcoming what he'd recognized as his eternal reward.

I, too, have done my best to live a life based on the teachings of God and the book that contains his sacred word. My faith had been passed down to me by my parents, local clergy, and twelve years of parochial education.

My belief in the one true God whose only son died for our sins was so ingrained into the fabric of my soul that I once quit my job, a union position with pension, because the office manager refused my request to let the pastor at my church come and serve communion at our staff Christmas party.

My commitment to the word of God was the reason I waited to experience intimacy until my wedding night. This faith is the basis of my opinion that life begins at conception, and that the integrity of that life holds greater value than a woman's right to choose. God's word informs me on what is and is not a sacred union between two individuals. These and other unpopular beliefs have not always served me favorably. They have cost me love relationships, friendships, and career opportunities. Yet, these are God's laws and I am a devoted child of my Creator.

One would expect that a woman of such faith would be at peace with her father's acceptance of the end of his life in this world. That woman might even find joy in her heart, knowing that her father is about to set forth on the journey toward rebirth and eternal life in God's Kingdom. While it's understandable that sadness would be part and parcel with the loss, her faith that an eventual reunion with her father in the Promised Land would at least provide a degree of solace.

What is hard to imagine is that this woman of great faith would bring legal action against the hospice that was set to assist her father in terminating his time in human form. One would be confused by this woman's attempt to prove that her father is not of sound mind and therefore incapable of being legally permitted to carry out this action.

I have read the King James Bible cover to cover. I have taught religious instructions to parish children after Sunday service. I can count at least a dozen times that I have stood at the altar before fellow members of my congregation and testified to my assurance of the existence of Almighty God with all of the conviction of someone affirming that the sun rises in the east and sets in the west.

Still, I was haunted by the notion that my father's decision to end his life and sit at the right hand of that same God was not based on his spiritual condition. Instead, it was a delusion born from a sickness of the mind.

I visited my father after he had learned of what I'd done to thwart his plan. He told me that he was hurt and confused. My father accepted his diagnosis as a sign that the Lord was calling him home. The continuing decline of his health was a clear message. It was obvious to my father that God had no intentions or expectations that he would carry on with a life bereft of any reasonable degree of usefulness and productivity. It was clear to him that his work in this dimension was complete. God was calling his child home. Committed to this belief, my father raised the question as to my right to interfere in our Creator's plan. The man, who raised me in a home where contradicting him was never well received, was appalled by the idea that I was questioning his rightness of mind.

His final thought on the matter was that my interference had nothing to do with my feelings on his faith. Instead, he assured me that it was a question regarding my own faith that led me to challenge the decision he made to cross over to the afterlife. The cold truth of that clear-minded observation was chilling.

For those who follow the same laws of God to which I subscribe, God is an all-or-nothing prospect. God is everything or nothing at all. As members of this faith, you're either in or you're out. But here I was, questioning whether there was some invisible line that separated deep faith and insanity. Or even worse, what if they are one and the same? That's the rub on faith, religion, and the place where each and every one of us stands on the concept of God. It all remains unknown. All that we have is what we believe.

Reluctantly, I withdrew my legal action on preventing my father from passing. He's gone, and the loss hurts. On top of that, I was left wondering whether I had made it possible for my dad to walk among the saints and angels, or did I cosign a mentally disabled man's suicide wish?

To help me through the mourning period, I've begun attending a bereavement prayer group led by Father Malley. I've gotten a great deal of comfort from his assurance that God never gives his children a load to bear that is more than we can handle. With God at my side, I will come out on the other end of my pain. Most of all, when I embrace the Father, Son, and Holy Spirit, I'm never alone.

Everything makes more sense to me when I trust in the idea that God is real. Whether I know that to be true, or need it to be true, I can't say.

Please don't ask me how I can worship and devote myself to a concept of a supreme being, make life decisions, and judge others by a set of laws that are meant to offer eternal life to those who follow them. Yet, when that faith is tested, I am plagued by a doubt strong enough to make me question the sanity of those very beliefs.

Does that make me a spiritual seeker, a hypocrite, or just a garden-variety human trying to make sense of what makes no sense?

If you're asking me, my guess would be all of the above.

THE ONE WHO CAME FROM ANGER

THE one who came from anger
    Walked in the devil's footsteps
Stared straight into the eclipse
And the sun, it left them blinded
It reminded them of iron
A blade stained with blood, and rusted
Ice-cold against pale flesh

The girl who knew no mercy
Sadistic in her manner
Set a trap for her Lord and Savior
And the Lord left her stranded
It returned her to the childhood
Knees against the church pew
Serving out her penance

A boy came from the forest
Tracked by the past and present
All of what he was and wasn't
And the future, it left him breathless
It lifted him in honor
A code not right to follow
So he choked on stolen valor

They blamed the womb that gave them life
They blamed the vine that shared their name

Raised a fist to the heavens and hell with rage
And cursed the demons who brought them shame

They put the blame on their skin
Put the blame on your skin
But never summoned their own reflection

DANIEL T BROWN

BESTS OF BOTH WORLDS

I GREW up on the Beatles. I lived and breathed the music and lives of the Fab Four. Believe me when I say that I am just as much in love with John, Paul, George, and Ringo today as I was the evening of February 9, 1964. This was the night that my family gathered in front of the black-and-white TV set in the living room, and I rested upon a couch pillow on the turquoise linoleum while Ed Sullivan introduced the lads from Liverpool to America.

George Harrison was, and continues to be, my favorite Beatle. He came across as so quiet and shy in the early days. I kinda saw him as somewhat disturbed. I think that was what I found so attractive about him. I thought that maybe if I could spend some time with George, I could fix him and make him happy.

I must have owned every magazine and newspaper clipping on the Beatles. I became somewhat obsessed. By the time "A Hard Day's Night" was in theaters, I knew everything there was to know about my idols. It was during this period that I first learned of Pete Best. He was the original drummer for the Beatles. Pete Best was fired from the band and replaced by Ringo Starr only months before the boys would begin topping the charts in England. Within a year of being out of the Beatles, his mates would rule the planet.

I didn't know what Pete Best looked like, nor had I ever heard the sound of his voice. Aside from him narrowly missing out on becoming a rock-and-roll god, I knew next to nothing about the man. But I felt sorry for Pete Best. As I grew and the quartet composed the soundtrack to my adolescence, I'd continue to wonder about Pete Best. What was it like for him to live his life as a footnote in the book of legends? Did it eat at him? Did he hate John, Paul, and George for stealing the fame and fortune that was within his grasp? Were there moments when the torment was so intense that the thought of ending it all was given more than a passing consideration?

It was around the time of the *Abbey Road* album that I first found myself taking an interest in the culinary arts. By the midseventies, I was ready to take the next step in higher education. I came to this decision while still coming to grips with the reality that John, Paul, George, and Ringo would forever be referred to as "former Beatles."

I committed to the road toward seriously pursuing my dream of becoming a chef. Correction: a world-famous chef. I was accepted into the New York Culinary Institute. With every moment I spent in the kitchen, I found myself falling deeper in love with edible artistry. Being the consummate overachiever, my dreams soon not only included being a master chef, but I had added internationally recognized restaurateur to the equation.

I was at the top of my class. Well, almost at the top. The only student whose kitchen mojo was superior to my own was Derek Leary. As far as social skills and having his shit together as a human being goes, Derek was a train wreck, but his dishes were pure masterpieces.

Much like my crush on the Beatle whose guitar gently wept, I was drawn to Derek's awkwardness. He became my drug of choice.

I worked my way into Derek's path and I discovered that taking the world of fine dining by storm was a dream we shared. In fact, this common bond was the main ingredient that held together the recipe for a love relationship between Derek and I that was heavily seasoned with tantrums, pettiness, and codependence on both ends.

However, our vision of ruling the culinary world made us blind to anything else. We ran ourselves ragged doing catering work and waiting tables. Every dollar we didn't need to survive was put away for what would be the launch of our joint venture into four-star dining.

At one of our catering events, we got turned onto Michelle and Russell. They were a husband-and-wife team of business majors from Columbia University. Derek and I began seeing them socially, and at one point, the idea of us all being partners was planted and took root.

Michelle, Russell, and I also had something in common that even Derek and I never fully shared: an obsessive love for the Beatles. One of the most bittersweet memories of my life was hanging out in the apartment that Derek and I rented, with Russell and Michelle the night of December 8, 1980. We sat in front of the TV in disbelief as the news of John Lennon's murder broke.

The next day, the four of us trekked to Central Park to mourn with the rest of the world. I sobbed in Derek's arms, and my heart knew emptiness as deep as any I had ever experienced. In an attempt to make something positive out of the situation, we decided that part of our healing should entail finally putting a location and name to our venture. The deal was made with swollen, teary eyes and our eight hands joined together. It was a very loving and positive moment. It felt so right.

We searched every square foot of Manhattan until we found the perfect place—an open retail space, the perfect size, just outside the meatpacking district. I suggested that we call the restaurant the Quarrymen. This was the name of the band John, Paul, and George were in before becoming the Beatles. As much as my three partners appreciated the sentiment, they hated the name. Michelle was mostly put off by the idea of "men" being in the title. Derek suggested that we drop the gender allegiance and just go with the Quarry. It rang true to us all, and we were on our way.

Our hearts were filled with love and good intentions, but our collective financial statement was a great distance from matching one of a restaurant investment group. In a sobering moment, the four of us decided to put the Quarry on the back burner for the time being. The plan was for Derek and I to finish paying off our student loans before we regrouped with Michelle and Russell to take another shot at opening the restaurant.

I was at my waitress gig one evening when Derek, Russell, and Michelle came to see me. They were elated. The trio pulled me outside to let me know that they had found an investor for the restaurant.

Lorilee Oneel came from some serious money. Her folks ran in the seven-figure circles, and Lorilee was looking to make her own mark in the business world. Michelle had a chance run-in with Lorilee at a political fundraiser event and she confided in her about our dream and dilemma. Lorilee wanted in.

The news that Lorilee had joined our group meant that the restaurant would become a reality. This was going to happen. On the downside, I didn't care for Lorilee's vibe one bit. Also, Lorilee was dead set against calling the restaurant the Quarry. Michelle, Derek, and Russell were willing to change the name if it meant keeping our investor. When that was brought to my attention, along with some other abrasive conditions that Lorilee insisted on before investing, I was beside myself. As much as we needed the money, I tried to convince the others that we should not let desperation water down our vision.

I asked the other three to break ties with Lorilee. I knew in my heart that the right investor was out there, the one who would be a better fit. We could have the Quarry and all that went along with it. Our dream on our own terms.

The plan was for all of us to take twenty-four hours to contemplate everything that was on the table. We'd regroup the following evening. The four of us were to meet up at a neighborhood diner to come to a consensus. When we met, I was surprised to see that Lorilee was also going to be a part of the meeting.

Lorilee's presence made it apparent that I had been outvoted. Before a word was uttered, I decided, after a quick inner dialogue between my pride and my ambitions, that I would wave the white flag and get with the program that was about to be presented. Michelle made it official when she spoke for the others. Lorilee was in the group.

I told Michelle that I understood and basically promised that I would get in line and keep my objections to myself. Then I jokingly added that I'd just have to get used to splitting our future fortune five ways rather than four. No one laughed at my stab at humor. I was about to learn that dividing money five ways, four ways, or any way, was not going to be an issue . . . for me.

Lorilee took control of the conversation. She acknowledged the friction and negativity that I had been directing her way during our team planning sessions. Lorilee agreed with my earlier assessment that this venture could never get off the ground as long as she and I were both members of the group. Since she was holding all the aces, it only made sense that I be the one to fold and cash in my chips.

To hear Lorilee take me apart like that in front of the people that I believed would have my back cut like a steel saber in my gut. The words ripped my flesh to shreds and freed my innards to wash across the table in a gushing tide of deep red blood.

At one point, I could not even hear what Lorilee was saying. My lasting mental image of the incident was of me fixed on Lorilee as she crushed my heart with her cold words. Her pale face wore the shittiest of shit-eating grins. I shot a quick look to Michelle and Russell, who were putting every effort into not making eye contact with me. As for Derek, the man who sat on the beach beneath the stars at my side on so many occasions as we planned a global conquest? He appeared to have checked his conscience and soul at the front door. To him, letting me, and all that was a part of us, go was a necessary evil. It was a sacrifice for his greater good. When the kill was complete, the predators made their exit, leaving me devastated and devoured.

I received a financial settlement for absolving my share of the partnership. In exchange for the buyout, I signed a document forfeiting my rights to take any legal action against my former partners.

It was enough for me to get my own small eatery up and running: Spanish and American fare in southeast Queens. For possible reasons, including poor location, oversaturation in the community, or my just sucking as a chef and business owner, I was shut down in less than two years' time.

It was within days of me filing my Chapter 11 claim that my former partners got their first cover story in *Food and Wine* magazine. I took the magazine off the rack at a street corner newsstand. The seething anger and jealousy that took hold of me is beyond description. My hands were shaking, and I imagined that these feelings were the same as what Pete Best experienced at first sight of the *Rubber Soul, Revolver,* or *Sgt. Pepper's Lonely Hearts Club Band* albums.

Based on the success of their initial New York restaurant launch, Michelle, Derek, Russell, and Lorilee opened a second location in Hollywood. They got gigs hosting parties for stars and major players in the movie and music business. The four of them had become celebrities in their own right. They were featured on talk shows in cooking segments. They did regular spots on the food and cooking networks. Good fortune led to their going international with a London location.

The final dagger to my heart came when I saw a piece on *Entertainment Tonight* about a private party for Paul McCartney that the group catered. Derek, Michelle, Lorilee, and Russell stood side by side with Sir Paul, bathing in the white of camera flash as I ate my heart out.

Filled with resentment, I first believed that they went out of their way to rub the spoils of their success in my face by working their way into the life of one of the Fab Four. It infuriated me. The torment only intensified when I was hit with the stinging realization that my former partners had most likely left me in their past long ago. Any thought of me and my feelings about their being in the presence of the cute Beatle never crossed their minds. To them, just like to the rest of the world, I was irrelevant.

The single-minded tireless pursuit of a dream that brought me to the edge of fortune and fame in my chosen field had turned to an obsession with thoughts of what damn well could have been.

Things got dark. I blamed the world for the life circumstance that was destroying me from the inside. When no one would accept the responsibility, I turned my anger toward God.

God, how could you? Why create a dreamer and not deliver on the dream?

Why turn the joy in my life to misery? Why take someone filled with the love of life and allow it all to turn black with hate? "God, I'll never forgive you" had become my refrain.

An early 2018 article in the *New York Times* broke the story about how Derek had been diagnosed with acute myeloid leukemia. Derek had returned to New York to undergo treatment. I felt the need to reach out and see if he would allow me to visit. My request went unanswered.

I wanted to see him and I needed to know. With death approaching Derek, I wanted to know if seeing him in his condition would alleviate the pain and jealousy I carried. My desire was to look into his eyes to see if Derek would feel regret for what he did to me. Maybe I would even get the sense that he was jealous of me. For simply outliving him, perhaps I was the winner.

What would it mean to Pete Best if he were to learn that John Lennon would have given it all back . . . every dollar, every moment, to trade places with Pete for the opportunity to continue to live? When John was taking his last breaths and the end grew near, do you think he would have traded lives with Pete if it meant that his existence would continue for at least another fifty years? Even if it meant never being an idol—no Yoko, no "Imagine," and no one to hear his cries to "Give Peace a Chance." Would Pete Best take that deal?

If I was faced with the decision to grab and hold all the success, money, and notoriety that I missed out on, for the price of taking Derek's place on his deathbed . . . would I? Is a dreamer's life, rich in fulfillment and contentment . . . the existence that I wanted so badly, worth more than life itself?

Following a lengthy pause, the best answer I could arrive at is, I don't know.

When I find myself in times of trouble, I pray that the answer will come to me and that the answer will set me free.

THE GARFIELD HORIZONS

MY attempts to establish an identity, and perhaps a degree of immortality, in high school led to failed campaigns for Garfield High School student body president and editor of the school news outlet. My plan to become captain of the cheer squad was dead on arrival when I didn't even survive the first cuts at tryouts.

The proposition of being just another face in the crowd in the class of 2003 was not an option. Desperate times called for desperate measures. I'd be the first to tell you that I never saw myself as the kind of girl who would be interested in making a run for homecoming queen. But in my senior year, I found myself throwing my hat in the ring.

Believe me, I was not under the delusion that I was pretty enough to be homecoming queen material. And though I bent over backward to be everyone's best friend, I was not a frontrunner for any kind of popularity contest. However, I had one thing going for me that made everything else irrelevant: I would be running unopposed.

At the turn of the twenty-first century, being voted homecoming king or queen was starting to lose its shine as far as being recognized as an "honor." In some of the neighboring counties, the high schools found the concept archaic and abandoned it all together, although there was still some cachet to the title at Garfield. In 1977, Maggie Foy was able to parlay being homecoming queen into a walk-on role in a Bedazzler commercial. If you google Maggie, she's also credited for appearing in two episodes of *The Facts of Life*. There's even a photo of Maggie with Charlotte Rae that was buried in the school's time capsule, which is set to be opened in 2061.

For me, the holy grail of becoming homecoming queen was that I would have my own full-page photo in the yearbook, *The Garfield Horizons*. If you can imagine, for eternity, when my classmates reflected on their history with a look through the Garfield Horizons Class of 2003, they would be reminded that Sheryl Canton was a big f-ing deal.

Upon making my candidacy official, I became obsessed with hanging banners and signs in the gym and hallways. I had my lips firmly planted on the homecoming committee members' asses. Now, all I had to do was show up at the big dance and claim my seat at the major players' table.

Believing that I had all the bases covered, I began my search for the perfect dress to go with my tiara, sash, and the smile on my face that was sure to communicate gratitude, reverence, and a taste of false modesty. The one thing I was not prepared for was Grace Delaney.

During one of my mad dashes after dismissal to remind fellow students to vote for me as they filed toward the exits, I found myself in a minor collision with a sheepish girl that I recognized from my trigonometry and home economics classes. She was several inches shorter than me, and though we were both seniors, her posture and plainness would make one think that perhaps she was a freshman if they didn't know better.

Then there's her legs.

Her legs were a distraction. Both knees seemed to be turned in on each other. The left shoe had a soul attached that was about four inches higher than the right, a compensation for the limb being much shorter than the other. Even with the corrective footwear, she walked with a very pronounced limp.

I apologized for the accidental run-in. She asked me, "Why the rush?" I offered the short, not too self-serving version of the story of my homecoming queen ambitions.

Grace Delaney was new to the school district. She had enrolled at Garfield for her senior year, and she was struggling to make friends and get involved in student activities. Grace asked if I needed help campaigning. She even offered to be my unofficial campaign manager. In return, I would introduce her to the homecoming committee and grease the wheels for Grace's attempts to widen her social circle. Grace and I would henceforth be friends.

My new amiga fell in well with the kids on the committee, and Grace thanked me profusely for helping her grow her friend garden. We would eat lunch together and chat on AOL messenger and on the phone almost nightly.

With the event nipping at our heels, Grace grabbed me outside of trig class. She was all juiced up and said that she wanted to share some news with me. Grace excitedly told me that the committee thought it would be a great idea if she entered the homecoming queen competition. Grace had discussed it with her guidance counselor and parents, and they all thought it would be good for her. Grace wanted to know what I thought of the idea.

"I think it's great, I wish you the best" was my response. Now, admittedly, those were the correct words to choose for my reply. However, the degree of sarcasm in which they were delivered did not evoke the spirit of love, friendship, and kindness.

Still, if I had left it at that. If I had just shown restraint, my remaining months at Garfield High School and beyond would have gone in a much more positive direction. But I got caught up in one of those moments when I just could not bring myself to close my mouth and walk away.

"Go ahead, see what happens," I continued. If that wasn't enough, I asked, "How could you do this to me?" before declaring that our friendship was over. Additionally, I made it clear to Grace Delaney that she was, as of that moment, dead to me.

You know, some years later during a therapy session, I was asked what I was getting out of reliving this story . . . retelling this tale over and over. Why was I still confessing so many years later? Was I sabotaging myself? Derailing relationships by painting myself as a villain?

We dug deeper and found that what I was searching for was simple forgiveness. Absolution. It was my subconscious hope that people would understand that I was young and believed that something to which I was entitled to was being taken from me.

Perhaps, rather than clutching your pearls and throwing stones at the monster who denied a vulnerable friend compassion at a time when compassion was called for, someone might choose to see the situation through my eyes. If you could forgive, maybe I could begin to forgive myself.

Maybe. If only what I've already confessed was the worst of what I'd done.

Immediately after Grace Delaney's reveal, I launched a plot of revenge. Garfield High had its own online group. It was mainly used for school notices, events, and activities. I created a fake account and began posting hurtful . . . hateful stuff about Grace. I used words like freak and ugly to describe her, and wrote that she didn't deserve our pity. I posted that allowing that limpy bitch to run for homecoming queen was an insult to our school and the entire Garfield County.

It was only a day or two later that Grace's parents were up at the school demanding that the perpetrator of this vile hate face justice. Principal

Adams launched an investigation, and it wasn't too long before I was being called out of class and escorted to her office.

Waiting for me there were my parents, Grace, and her parents. On my way to face my accusers, I had made a commitment to myself that I would lie and deny to the end. Yet, the looks of disappointment and anger that I encountered on the faces of my mother and father immediately broke me to pieces. I offered a complete confession with little prodding from anyone.

Grace and I were excused from the room as the principal and our parents discussed my fate. We sat in silence outside the door as guilt and remorse ran through me until I succumbed to the need to try to make things better.

"I'm sorry," I said to Grace in a low and sorrowful voice. I was unable to turn my head to face her. Feeling the need to explain, I offered, "I never should have made this contest about your disability, but . . ."

Grace cut me off and came back at me with words that put the entire incident into perspective. "You wanted to make this contest about my disability. Instead, you made it about yours."

We returned to silence, until our jury appeared and the verdict was handed down. I would not be expelled, as Mr. and Mrs. Delaney had originally requested. For my sins, I would be disqualified from the homecoming queen competition. I was also banned from attending the dance altogether.

For me, there would be no tiara and no sash. My dress would be returned unworn. After dismissal, I was instructed to take down every sign and banner. I lost count of how many laughs and whispers I heard behind my back from students and school staff who took a moment to stop and witness my shame as I carried my collection of useless posters to the dumpster bin that was left for me by the school custodian.

I was accepted to a college in the Midwest and moved out there permanently after graduation. When the invitation for the Garfield High class of '03 ten-year reunion arrived in my inbox, I pretended that I never received it.

On occasion, I'll blow the dust off my copy of the Garfield Horizons. I turn to the full-page picture of Grace Delaney, the 2003 homecoming queen. I imagine that one day, I will see her again. When I do, I'll thank her for the friendship and companionship that she offered me. I'll tell her how proud I am to have known her. I'll let her know that even when I was trying to tear her down, I was in awe of the greatness of her strength and beauty. A strength and beauty that I hope one day to aspire to.

When I see her, I'll be seeking absolution.

TO THOSE WHO LOVE

F OR those of us who love with abandon, love recklessly . . . without fear . . . without caution. We have known heaven, though we have also known the true hell of heartache.

There's a man I love. I am drawn to his smell, moved by his voice . . . the pattern of his walk. His name is Joelle. His cubicle is the length of the hallway from the one I occupy in the accounts payable suite.

Don't ask me if I'm sure if it's love. I'm old enough and have been around long enough to know. It is love—pure and absolute. Does Joelle love me? I've learned that sometimes, love is far too complicated for a yes-or-no answer. Yes, he does love me. He will love me.

He'll know it in his heart . . . when we meet. When the opportunity to break our office anonymity at last presents itself. We will advance beyond polite smiles and nods when passing through corridors or on elevator rides. When Joelle is permitted to place the face with the name he's been kind enough to include in each of his all-staff emails.

From there, what Joelle and I experience will be so much more than just cavalier and careless sex. That's right. Sex. Would you believe me if I said that Joelle and I have been intimate? I wouldn't lie about a thing like that. He doesn't know. I mean, he knows what he's done. He just doesn't know that I am the object of his lusting.

Through no fault of my own, I recovered his cell number when I was perusing coworker's files and applications in a private moment. I was the last to leave the office that night. The night of Sara Brauer from HR's baby shower. After rushing to CVS for a throwaway phone, I sat outside the station at Broadway Junction. I was high on the anticipation of the start of a new relationship. You know the feeling.

What love of food, movies, and art would connect us? Which of my summer dresses would Joelle declare his favorite? The one he'd ask me to wear when we'd meet on the ferry dock, walk back to my place for dinner, and . . . who knows?

With shaky fingers, I punched in ten digits. "Hello," Joelle answered on the second ring in a tone that was more formal than friendly. That scared me. "Hello?" Joelle repeated. Followed by, "Who's calling?" A response to my silence.

I swallowed hard and forced a reply. "Sorry, I may have dialed the wrong number," I muttered in retreat, downing in the moment. "No need to be sorry," Joelle spoke in a voice that exhibited a disarming, even a touch inviting, change in his demeanor.

I felt a bit of my confidence returning. "Really? That's very kind of you," I said. "We can talk if you'd like," Joelle replied. "Would you like that?" The conversation had crossed into the flirtatious. It wasn't very long before we were engaged in talk of a graphically sexual nature. Plans were made for me to call again.

No names were exchanged. No stories shared. Just raw energy. A primal connection.

Calls began once a week. Soon enough, it was two, three . . . even four times. Each conversation pushed the limits of lust and decency. Our exchanges ran the gamut from the romantic to engaging in acts that were completely out of bounds for my liking. But I put up little resistance. It had been my experience that a girl needs to step outside her comfort zone from time to time in the bedroom to maintain her man's attention.

Some might see my giving consent to something in which I was opposed to morally as a show of weakness. To me, I was flattered that Joelle cared enough to take me into the dark corners of his fantasies. These were things he swore he could never tell anyone else. That was proof enough to me that what we had was real.

For boys, it's all about a good time and putting off what's meaningful. They'll do it indefinitely if you don't put your foot down. Neither Joelle nor I are getting any younger. If we were going to begin our life together, plan our future . . . our family, I felt it was time to take the next step.

For this important conversation to take place, it was necessary for me that Joelle feel that he was in comfortable and familiar surroundings. To me, it only made sense that I meet Joelle at his apartment for this serious, cards-on-the-table talk. To make this happen, the only sensible thing for me to do was to follow Joelle home on the subway after work and approach him at his doorstep.

On a wintry Wednesday evening, I trailed Joelle to the 23rd Street station. It took some doing, but we boarded the train car simultaneously three doors apart. He remained unaware of my presence.

As the train crept into 50th Street, Joelle stood up and approached the exit. As the doors parted, we stepped off the train. Joelle turned and began taking steps toward the stairs to the street. I matched his stride from a safe distance.

At the foot of the steps, a strange woman approached Joelle and rushed into his arms. Joelle returned the embrace. The hands of this woman clutched at the back of his coat. Catching my eye, a diamond worn on her right ring finger.

Joelle and this other woman proceeded up the stairs, holding hands. Tears filled my eyes as the wind stirred by the departing train blew my hair forward, into my face, mercifully blocking my view of his blatant betrayal.

What do we do, those of us who love so fearlessly, when infidelity makes its presence known? All I can tell you is that my love is unconditional, that my love knows forgiveness.

Our phone calls continue to this day. I stand by Joelle, and I accept the responsibility of offering him the release and satisfaction that he clearly is not afforded by . . . her.

When anger and jealously get the best of me, I think about how sweet and attentive Joelle is out at the park, or at the beach, with his little girl. A child. When he and that woman take this child out to ride on the swings or walk by the ocean, I see Joelle at his best . . . as what he is meant to be. This child, her name is Agnes. The daughter of his mistress. When I watch them together in the evening or on a Saturday, I imagine what joy will come when Joelle and I have Agnes and raise her as our own flesh and blood.

How can this woman carry on like she does and see herself fit for motherhood? Joelle won't stand for it. I won't have it. The judge will see what's right. Joelle and I will walk off into the future. Agnes will take my hand. She will know my love. She will call me mom.

Very soon, I will reveal myself and my intentions to Joelle. One day, very soon. He will reciprocate and take joy in discovering that his one true love was waiting for him just a few feet away. Close enough to reach out and feel.

I've heard it said that you should love like you'll never be hurt. That's so childish. It hurts. Sometimes, love hurts so bad. But when you find true love, the one-in-a-million love, like the love that Joelle and I share . . . it's all worth it. It really is.

DANIEL T BROWN

Don't worry, Joelle, I'm coming . . . coming for you. It would be foolish to resist, to deny yourself the joy of everlasting love. I'm coming for you. Why resist? There will be no more denial . . . no more rejection. I won't have it. I won't allow it. Don't worry about a thing. I'm here now.

I'M STEPPING OVER

FROM this day forward, my name is the Liberated
The beat of my unclaimed heart is syncopated
This desire for my freedom cannot be overstated
My elated is underrated
And this cannot be debated

A crown of thorns for my emancipation
One giant step outside the regulation
Pay my share for this cohabitation
If you chase me to the station
I will grant you visitation

I'm stepping over
The man that sleeps outside my door
He asked for five, and I gave four
But just as long as he doesn't snore
I'm stepping over

Let's break out of this charming institution
Pillow talk to start a revolution
Front-row seat for my daily execution
Solution to my retribution
For a falling institution

On the dance floor with glowing sticks and man buns
Posting pics with selfie sticks and handguns
Late-night eating with beef lo mein and wonton
Son, this is what we call fun
Living like we're still young

I'm stepping over
The man who's got the antidote
Says life is hard so be cutthroat
But he's no good, 'cause he doesn't vote
I'm stepping over

Brass-knuckled justice, the kids—they call it retro
The lower we sink, the higher and higher we go
Personal foul, possession, and a free throw
Follow me to the freak show
Mi nombre es el diablo

Lawbreaking, deal taking every time the rent's due
My head's in a vice and frozen like an igloo
Another brick wall we're gonna have to break through
Take a cue from my clue
I love you means I hate you

I'm stepping over
The man who says that he's the lord
But he's not falling on his sword
Still, he insists that I'm the fraud
I'm stepping over

WITH GRATITUDE

I AM grateful to the wonderful people who agreed to appear on the cover of this book:

Alyssa Romano

Zepe

Jessica Parrish

Elasea Douglas, singer of Acute Inflections

Patty Bobo

Also, thank you, Patty, for putting up with me and encouraging me when I decide to indulge my need to create. I love you.

Thank you, Paul Gambino, for helping me shoot the cover and bring the concept to life.

Special thanks to the people at Xlibris for taking me through the publishing process with respect and kindness.

Much thanks to every person I have met in my life. In some way, shape, or form, you have influenced the stories contained in these pages. You are my who, what, where, when, and sometimes why.

Most of all, thank you to everyone who took the time to read this book. I am forever grateful